I0588423

Underland Arcana finds a crack and burrows deep, seeking a dark spot to curl up and wait out the winter months. There, we shall read stories about household appliances, BBQ, and what we make when we are allowed to tinker in the garage. Stories about hell rides, stories about things behind glass, and stories about the hopes we have for the future.

This issue completes the second year of Underland Arcana, and finds us in a very strange mood indeed.

Underland Arcana is published on a seasonal basis. This issue is published in conjunction with the autumn equinox as the night slips past the day and the moon spreads out across the sky.

EDITOR
Mark Teppo

COVER IMAGE
cranach / stock.adobe.com

SIGIL ART
Andrew Penn Romine

PUBLISHER
Underland Press
Clackamas, OR, USA

Look, there. See how the lights move . . .

https://www.underlandarcana.com

UNDERLAND
ARCANA

~ 08 ~

Underland Press

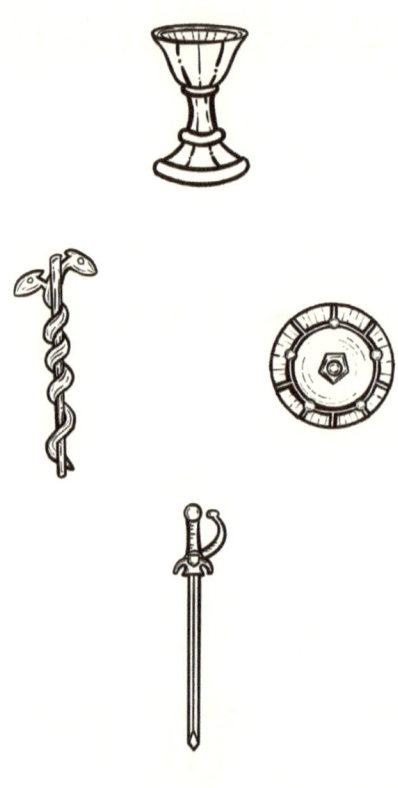

Contents

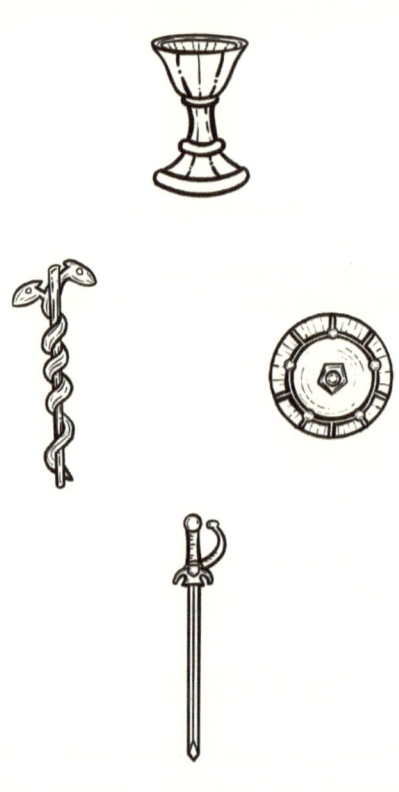

The Road Show

This one was a little different. It came out a month earlier than usual, and it had several stories I actually solicited for the issue. Why? Because we were debuting two Underland titles (Darin Bradley's *Bloodmetal* and Bonnie Jo Stufflebeam's *Glorious Fiends*) at Dan's Silverleaf in Denton, TX, that September. When you do a reading at Dan's, you try to make it a little more rock and roll than just a bunch of folks hiding behind microphones. So, I needed an opening act, who were going to be the "Arcaneers."

Which led to sourcing some local talent. I did have one story already lined up from someone who lived within driving distance, and I reached out to a few others who might be available and asked if they wanted to be part of the "band," as it were. Delightfully, they said 'yes,' and that's how we ended up with a handful of local authors at a reading, who were all supporting new titles on the table.

In fact, it was a bit of an 'aha!' moment. I've reached that point where, yes, I could source content, do editorial and production, and have a book on the table for a well-represented showing, and it would all look like magic.

We did it again with the *Cozy Cosmic* anthology, and we took that band on the road. Okay, so it was only one show, but there was a van and some howling (er, singing) in the night.

Either way, issue 8 of *Arcana* was a milestone in some ways, and not because it was the best-dressed of the lot. Enjoy the stories.

Mark Teppo
Oct 12th, 2022

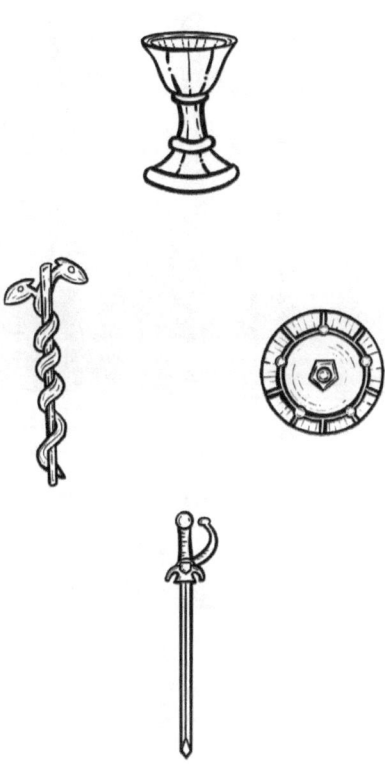

Proof of Stake

~ *D. T. O'Conaill*

The following represents the most up to date compilation of information available on the clearnet surrounding the token known as $STOKR. The below is not intended to be considered as an exhaustive source of knowledge on this asset, nor are any of the statements contained therein to be considered as an endorsement of the return prospects of investment in this token. Given the fragmentary nature of this collection of documents, reflective of the generally fragmentary nature of knowledge about this token, the author cannot advise any specific action in regards to fund or capital engagement with this asset at present. The below represents due diligence undertaken on behalf of the DeSelby Fund incorporated in Hybrasil and is not intended as advisory to the aforementioned or any other fund, trader or entity.

⊙

"StokerLabs, and its premier decentralised financial product $STOKR, represent a new frontier in the world of defi that combines ground-breaking technological development, prosaic insight into the pur-

pose and nature of human consciousness and pri-
vacy-tools in order to revolutionise the landscape of
blockchain-assisted task scalability. $STOKR as an
asset finds the heart of its innovation in its quality
of telescopy: it moves from macro to more granular
modalities with unprecedented efficiency, bringing
together transanglospheric financial footlooseness
with a distinctly wry attitude peculiar to our own
small north Atlantic island."

—**An excerpt from the $STOKR white paper**

"Wen this thing gonna 10X Ive got a fat sack to
build my apocalypse bunker w"

—**Transcribed from a screenshot taken in a
private telegram channel for $STOKR investors**

"Much has been written about just how plagued the
emergent world of "decentralised finance" is with
scams of all varieties. So called "rug pulls" and the
endless proliferation of derisively named "shitcoins"
have been one major consequence of this brand new
technological space and its minting of overnight
millionaires. Just as hyped up scams are predictably
endemic to such a new and ever-altering technological space, so too is the rejoinder that every upcom-
ing project hyped into existence promises to bring
us something "radically new and never before seen."
Whether by the alchemy of jamming together previously existed buzzwords into unusual combinations

or plucking neologisms of their own out of thin air each and every new token that blackens the skies of our feeds seems to desperately screech and crow about its own novelty. But $STOKR is the real deal. But if "advanced technology" and the "metaverse" and "quantum blockchains" have become worn cliches coming from crypto developers themselves, then no doubt hard-nosed and breathless declaration of a token's technological "real deal" status are a cliche of crypto-watcher blogs like mine. But this time it's the real thing. For serious guys"

—**Excerpt from an archive of the Medium page of an individual using the penname MachineOfLovingGrace**

As should be evident from these snippets the problem of understanding the nature of the $STOKR token is besieged not only by its own idiosyncratic nature but also the general "crypto-haze" endemic to its form. Its promoters speak in generalities as jargon filled as they are fantastic and its loud supporters take up detractors' claims of the commodity as a "cult" with great and unironic enthusiasm. While the latter is the case with many in the space of so-called "Decentralised Finance" the holders and boosters of $STOKR embody this mindset in a far more elaborate and theatrical way as they have molded their communities and rituals on a variety of pre-Christian mystery religions of the ancient world. Smaller investors are referred to as "initiates" while more established investors, especially those either directly related to the developers themselves or involved in sub-communities that interpret and catalogue the actions of developers and the token's place in the broader economy, gain the title of "hierophant."

The above extracts involve contributions from, in order, the developers, an initiate and a moderately-well known hierophant. Given the consistency of standard crypto-space jargon across each excerpt we would not ordinarily suggest a stake in this token as an ongoing concern for the fund but further research has suggested to us that the clearnet and mainstream social communications of $STOKR boosters represent a deliberate strategy of occlusion on their part. What follows is more indicative of the substance of the community and the investment opportunity it might represent. Read on at your own risk. Invest carefully. Do not get captured.

> *"My thanks to Hierophant E and Hierophant σ for assisting myself and other new initiates in explicating the nature of the value stored within and represented by our tokens. Each day our understanding grows more full and rich and the true potential of this metatechnological feat becomes less and less opaque. The cult now sees plainly the hidden hands that operate behind the to-ings and fro-ings of this world and sees it fit to seize them with fits. We are but one rung up the ladder of paralysing the Powers That Be. Let us endeavor each day to climb one more higher."*

—Initiate Foxtrot, who has been linked to the clearnet personality of AdmiralSenzu88, speaking on one of the $STOKR communities on the custom MeshNet.

"The following coordinates have encoded our security for this session. 53°38'01.0"N 7°41'09.8"W. 53°40'16.8"N 9°03'49.8"W. 52.222166, -7.760268. This portion of the arcane working is locked into the firmament on the basis of the keys placed in the previously mentioned sites. These sacrifices provide stability to the chain and liquid value to our universe. We thank the brave initiates for the quality of their staking."

—Hierophant Ж, speaking of vital 'burial keys' at a meeting hosted at a location which we cannot disclose and which does not, in the traditional sense, exist.

"Holy shit are we going to be the official Crypto token of the Bram Stoker Festival in Dublin!! Time for this thing to go to the MOOOOOOOOOOOOOOOOOOON"

—@KingCong/Moon4Sam, a minor Twitter crypto personality

As should be evident from the above excerpts the nature of the $STOKR token is far more arcane and involved than the usual crypto-space bloviating about advanced technologies and new paradigms of financial technology. Although the space of cryptocurrency and associate technologies contains much of its own in-jargon and feverish, cult-like atmospheres the $STOKR token community truly embraces these elements and takes them to the nth degree. The Bram Stoker Festival, based in Dublin, has denied any connection to and knowledge of the $STOKR crypto token following a number of inquiries. In this regard, as many others in its surface communiques and those portions of its that peak out like iceberg tips from the clearnet, $STOKR resembles other cryptocurrencies that "pump" on the basis of partnership rumours that never come to fruition. However the fact that at least two unidentified bodies have been discovered in the locations marked in the above communication as 'key sites' points to something that stakes out $STOKR as a radically departure from its contemporaries. This makes it a fertile investment opportunity for movers with the mind and the stomach for such growth possibilities.

> *"We are bonded in wood and blood. These are the oldest measures of values and, according with the circular notion of technological time that has been revealed to us, shall also be the future of our value system. We are staked by flesh and the spooling out of arterial systems like the pulling of a thread to unravel the substance of the world-order. The old flesh is the new technology. The old blood is the new currency. HODL $STOKR"*

—Entitled "Summation of \$STOKR value set/ White Paper 2.8" this was found on a scrap of paper tucked into an empty jewel case tapped to the back of an iron girder in the unfinished site of the Parkway Valley Shopping Centre Development, Limerick, Ireland

A dispassionate review of the broad range of materials surrounding this token suggests an investment opportunity both risky and compelling. Our due diligence complete on behalf of the DeSelby Fund the authors would like to full-throatedly endorse the fund take up a substantial position in this token. By any means necessary.

A Random Aquarium at the Pier

~ Joshua Flowers

You stretch your tiny arms past the edge of the pier as an Atlantic wind billows your sundress. Beneath you, waves hit the thick, barnacled pillars of the pier with all their force, yet you feel no shaking. No one atop the busy tourist space seems worried about the sea's casual wrath.

A finger snaps for your attention, but you don't respond fast enough. Your mother yanks your hand into hers, her grip too tight, as she scans over the crowd on tiptoes. Her heavy purse dangles at the crook of her bronze elbow. She wears a white sundress similar to yours, but that is an accident. When she bought it for you months ago, she was too tired to notice she bought you a smaller version of something she already owned.

"Fucking place," she whispers under her breath. You hear the swear but say nothing. Even you, for all your childish faults, can tell your mother needs a moment out of the sour, sweat-soaked air and noisy groupings of tourists. She needs somewhere dark where she can close her eyes, knock her head back, and take a deep shot of breath.

She decides on a destination and drags you. The fingers hooked into your wrist hurt. Not enough to bruise (not yet) but enough to notice. Poor child. You know your mother doesn't mean it, so you're trying hard to just be thankful she is spending her one day-off with you. Instead of sleeping, she's exploring a pier she hates because you once mentioned over diner that you'd like to visit it.

The two of you move towards an uninteresting building laid next to others like a brick laid into a wall. The name escapes you as a pair of women in wide-brim hats obscure the sign above the door. Years later, when you have grown into the shape of your mother, you will tell your story to other girls grown into mothers, and they won't believe you. You won't believe you. That'll drive you a little mad, but that's alright. That's what childhood memories are meant to do.

In the present, your mother lets go inside the dimly lit lobby. You find a seat on a bench bathed in neon as she for tickets. Your pink sneakers clash against the blue and black swirls of the carpeted floor. Whatever this place is, they regularly vacuum as it's all too clean for the pier. Mother returns with two tickets: they have ghostly faces stamped above the word "ADMISSION."

"Where are we?"

"Who knows, but it's got air conditioning." Your mother takes a deep breath. The cool lighting is enough to hide her burnt cheeks. She notices your apprehension. "It'll be fun. Come on."

You follow her further in. Truthfully, you would have liked to listen to the waves a little longer, but the money is already spent, so you keep your mouth shut. Besides, following at the heels of mothers is what children do.

Through a large pair of doors (one blue, one black) you find a man in a gaudy suit blocking your way. He greets you both with a deep bow and has the air of a theatre villain. A man of big monologues who is killed at the end by a simple kick.

"Welcome," he says in a deep voice, "To my Aquarium of Horrors!"

First Exhibit—The Phantasmal

Pickled Screams

The tank is bright red and lights you in the color of a blood bath. The guide reads aloud from a notecard he produces from his jacket pocket. "Most screams can be pickled. All you need is the right apparatus, and a tank filled with special soul-absorbing jelly. Screams, being a shed part of the soul, usually dissipate in the air within moments, but the jelly prevents that dull end. If you bring your face close, you can see them bounce from wall to wall."

With a smile, the guide gestures his white hand to the glass. You crane your neck back at your mother. She is near the entrance, raising an eyebrow at the sight. Her eyes lock with yours, and you can tell she wants to say, "It's alright hun. You can get close," but she hesitates. Her phone buzzes, and now that it's in her hand, you know the words won't come. She'll ignore you until she's ready.

The guide gestures again towards the tank. Mustering a little courage, you step up. The red glow is soft on your eyes. Staring inside is like peering into a massive block of strawberry jelly.

A foggy face presses against the glass in front of you with a soft thump. Their eyes are twisted and mouth wide in a scream. The face pulls away. Somewhere you can't see, another thump.

You flinch.

You didn't mean to, but you did. The guide saw.

The Drowned Man

Two spotlights illuminate a phony seafloor of foam. A pale white man is inside, sitting on a cheap fold-out chair. His shirtless body is bloated, and thin weeds of hair float above his mostly bald top.

"Does a drowned man need much explanation?" The guide says with a soft, solitary chuckle.

The drowned man turns towards you, but you can tell he sees nothing. His eyes are foggy white orbs. He's like dad back when he used to live with you, too drunk to see anything more than shapes. You glance at your mother, wondering if she notices too, but she's still on her phone. She hasn't pulled her face up since the screams.

A Prophecy

Lights swirl around the center of the tank, twisting water in a dazzling display that catches your breath. Suddenly this strange trip is worth it.

"Sailors of olde would look for these out at sea. They'd bring their boats beside the churning light and toss a man down. If he came back up, he'd return with a new heading towards glory."

You step closer, wanting to press your face to the glass like the pickled screams. Inside the light, you think you see yourself but older. The glass keeps you too far away to view clearly. There is so much you can't tell. Are you beautiful? Are your father and mother nearby, or are you alone? The light gives you no answers. You want to get closer to it. Enveloped by it. Maybe then you would understand.

"Careful," the guide says. You glance up at him. Something about his over-the-top persona keeps you on edge. "It is easy to get lost in a prophecy of the future. Usually, it's of such amazing quality, one would forget they had to ever trudge through a less elegant past to reach their revelation."

From the corner of your eyes, you see your mother finally put away her phone. She still lingers at the edge of the exhibit with a dull-eyed stare. You suspect she wasn't even listening to the guide. Part of you wants to beg her over, afraid she might miss your dazzling future. Another part of you—the selfish, evil part of you that would wake your poor, overworked, exhausted mother from a nap demanding food and love—says, *Keep this for yourself. She doesn't care.* It is a petty kind of revenge. New to you, but one you'll understand better as you grow older.

When you turn back to the light, you see the specter of yourself walking alone. She is in some kind of large, empty space (for a moment, you think a field), and the moon hangs low in a daylight sky. There is something off about this older you, but the prophecy is too hazy to tell what.

Transfixed, you think about standing in the spot forever, waiting to see the final destination of your future self. Maybe then you'll finally understand why this vision is so important. Why it grips you so strongly.

"What happens if someone stays in the light too long?" you ask, feeling a sting from your dry eyes. You've forgotten to blink.

The guide smiles. "Don't you remember the last display?"

Second Exhibit—The Mawcillious Murderers

Congo Teeth Fish

Lime green lights illuminate the rocky tank. Its floor is decorated with plastic gold and toy skulls. Above the gaudy display, rows of teeth swim back and forth on tiny, red fins. Each tooth is the shape of a porcupine quill curved behind the body of the fish. Ironically, you can't actually see their mouths. The teeth get in the way.

"The Teeth Fish are a rare breed that only exist in one, large lake in the Congo. The locals took great care to preserve the population as they subsist on a very meaty diet. Funnily enough, these hungry fish are not ones for cannibalism. Perhaps they find one another too difficult to chew?" He chuckles then checks his watch. "Look at that. Feeding time."

A worker tosses hunks of cow into the tank. The clear water turns a messy, transparent red. Teeth swarm the meat and tear it apart in a feast so thorough they lick the blood from the water. In a blink, the tank is clean again like nothing happened. Just a tank full of teeth swimming about.

Maine Knife Lobsters

You ask your mother what she thought of the fish.

"It was a little dark," she admitted, "But as long as you're enjoying yourself."

You say nothing. It takes a few more steps before your mother thinks to ask if you are enjoying yourself instead of presuming like she often does. As you answer, the next display greets you with angry smashes against glass.

You hear them before you see them. Their massive claws are as large as your head with white tips that darken into nightshade shells. The color just barely hides the lobster's furious, pearl-shaped eyes. There are four in the tank, and when they see you, they go into a frenzy. Their attack is furious as they stab, as they pinch, as they want desperately to rip you down to the marrow of your bones.

The guide pulls out a notecard and starts to speak, but you can't hear what is said of them over their infuriated drumming. It occurs to you that your mother probably didn't hear your answer either. She says nothing about it, so you do likewise.

☉

Coral Dragons

The name stirs a fantastical hope in you. Dragons? Here? They're real? You feel like the main character of a fantasy book, about to discover the beginnings of a magical adventure.

Your smile fades when you see them. They look like sea horses, but instead of flowery limbs, these dragons have coral spirals shaped like buttercream frosting flowers. The fish don't swim but hop across the sandy floor in spasmodic jerks. They float from one spot to the next as if pretending to swim and failing.

Nothing in this exhibit captivates you. Your mother stands by a corner, rubbing the dried sweat from her face. She closes her eyes like she's trying to beckon a quick moment of sleep. You've never seen anyone sleep while standing up (like you've never seen teeth fish, lobsters, or dragons before today), but if anyone could do it, it's your mother.

This is the first day off she's had in weeks. After this, she goes back to work at the midnight shift. You know it's likely Granma will put you to bed again when you get home, but maybe if you sleep in late, you might wake up with your mother in her bed. You could sneak into her arms. Snuggle beneath them. Pretend she had never left at all.

☉

Third Exhibit—The Horrors

The Dredge

At first, you think it looks like an octopus. A very thin, very sickly-looking octopus. When you count the tentacles, you realize there are too many, then think it resembles more a floating patch of seagrass. In the shaggy, flowing mass, you see something beneath. A boney, withered arm. You blink, and it vanishes in the shuffle of tendrils.

"There are maybe two hundred Dredges in the world. They roam the ocean floor as if searching for something, but no one knows what. In all observation, no one has ever seen them eat, yet they do hunt. A Dredge will grab fish and smash their heads against the nearest rock. They'll let their dead prey float in the water and move on, perpetually continuing their search. Sometimes unlucky explorers will swim too close to them. They often end up like the fish."

As you stare, a boney foot like a burned-up skeleton appears before disappearing again. It takes you too long to realize the creature isn't swimming but walking. In the sand, you can see the marks of the shriveled tentacles dragging behind. There are no footprints.

Your mother steps up behind you. "This one kind of reminds me of your father," she says as a little joke, but you don't laugh. This isn't the one that reminded you of your father. She hadn't been paying attention for that one. Noticing she has a little more peppiness now that you're both somewhere cool, you decide to leave that annoyance behind. This is your favorite version of your mother: the one that has the energy to give you attention.

The two of you stare at the Dredge for a long while (to the irritation of the guide who wishes to move onto his next horror), and each of you guesses a thing it might be looking for. Treasure. Friends. Cigarettes. A drink. The principal's office--you say this one and your mother laughs, remembering the time she needed twenty minutes to find the parent-teacher meeting. Family.

Both your jokes die off from boredom as you realize the Dredge has been simply walking in circles this entire time.

The Discarded Warrior

They look like a knight but not. They're a fish. Kind of? It has a thick tail and two arms, both poking out a round shell. The shape is awkward as if it's hunched inside. You can't tell if it has a human head or fish head beneath. Somehow it sees you then swims to a corner. You hear crying as if someone was sobbing right by your shoulder.

"What you see is a thing from an ancient race that took up war against an even older enemy. Unsurprisingly, they lost. Their war had been needless and futile, ending in a defeat so thoroughly gruesome, each subsequent generation only knew how to cower."

The thing breaks off a sharp shard from a corner of its shell and tries to stab itself through the chest, but the shell blocks the blow. The crying intensifies, and you realize you've never seen something so large cry. Not an adult. Not your mother nor father. After a certain age, you expect people to forget how. This unhealthy notion will be reinforced when your Granma passes and your mother will be too proud to show her tears. That will be hard, but not nearly as hard as when your father swerves into a canal. For that death, your mother will dance with revelry.

At the display, your mother is bothered by the stabbing. You can see her hand twitch to shield your eyes but stop because she knows you've already seen too much. Trying to protect you now would be silly.

Once the shard of shell shatters in the creature's hand, it tumbles over the sand to get to the other corner. It breaks off a new piece and returns to attacking itself.

The guide shakes his head. "It's all for show. If it truly wanted to end things, it would. Even the most pitiful of us can think of at least one way to the grave."

The Visitor

They dance the way only things that swim can. Six fins entwined within one another push the creature up to the top of the tank before it spins above—showing off dazzling, orange scales—then dives down. With a twirl, it stops itself from smashing against the steel floor. They hadn't bothered to put up any flourishes in the tank. No illusions to distract from the fact this is a beautiful thing inside a cage.

The guide tells you he knows nothing of the Visitor, just that they aren't from your world. You think he's lying. The fish appears normal albeit strange. It's like a giant goldfish, a size between you and your mother. The size of an older sibling.

As you move, The Visitor follows, dragging itself against the glass to get closer to you. You put a hand where its body would be, and it spins in delight. Your mother pulls out her phone to get a video, but the guide blocks her. He reminds her that there are no pictures or recordings allowed in his aquarium.

They both look away as The Visitor folds its fins over the glass where your hand touches. You think the fins resemble the ribbons on your school's maypole piled atop the ground. You can see something stir beneath.

It stings your palm through the glass, and you jump back. Neither the guide nor your mother notice, still arguing about the picture policy. You shake out your hand, and the pain vanishes. There is no mark on the glass. Your palm appears fine. The orange thing dances excitedly as you move on. All the while, your mother complains about being unable to capture the memory.

☉

Special Exhibit

The hallway curves as if you've reached the end, yet the guide brings you to one last thing: a rickety, steel plate cage dangling from a chain above a pit. He opens it and gestures inside. "We have a special exhibit under construction, though considering what wonderful guests you've been, I thought you might enjoy a glimpse."

Your mother places both hands on your shoulder as if ready to pick you up and carry you away. The guide sees this but doesn't take it personally. To show you it's safe, he steps inside the cage first then twists around the empty space.

Still unsure, your mother looks to you, lets you decide. Deep inside your soul, something beckons you to see what's next in a language you don't know but think you could pronounce if you tried. A meeting that almost feels like fate. A name half-noticed further down the page by a wandering eye.

You shrug, and your mother takes this as affirmation for one last horror. The two of you step into the cage with the guide. The door shuts on its own, and the cage lurches downward like an elevator. The soft neon that had accompanied you the entire time fades as you sink into a pit of shadows. The cage drops fast enough for you to feel it in your stomach. It's tough to keep your pink sneakers steady.

The cage slows and gently settles atop a bed of sand in a pitch-black room. You can't see the edges of the walls or ceiling. Only dark abyss. The cage opens, and the guide shows you out.

"Don't wander away. We wouldn't want you two getting lost."

Ortro

The guide says nothing more. He stands with his hands behind his back, gazing at the distance. You stare too yet see nothing. A long time passes, and your mother asks if maybe you should leave. You ask for five more minutes. After coming this far, you want to see this last thing.

Six glowing eyes open in the air a great distance away, and you realize you're not in a room. What exists around you is a sky without stars and a horizon that never knew light. The six blue-light eyes, positioned like a spider's, don't illuminate its own body well. The head is like a sea-rotted cube that has eaten off its own corners atop a too-thin neck that disappears into the abyss. The lights face you. Stare back at you. For minutes, you try to decipher the rest of its body through the dark but cannot. In a blink, the eyes inch closer.

"We should go," your mother says, a rattle in her voice. You and her look back. The guide is gone. The opened cage remains.

When you check on the eyes, they are far too close. They loom like a set of blue suns. You still can't see what kind of body the neck leads to. Your mother grabs you by the wrist and drags you back into the cage.

The door shuts.

The cage goes up.

Your mother shifts her hands over yours then squeezes.

As you fly away, the eyes follow. They keep pace. Between the two, you worry the cage is slower even though your guts strain from its momentum. You expect a shadow drenched limb to appear from the darkness to smash you apart.

Despite your fears, you see nothing. Only the eyes.

They don't shrink as if you've outrun them but blink out one by one. You and your mother are in pure, total, heavy darkness for but a moment before the cage pulls itself back up into an aquarium flooded by neon.

You're at the end, and a nice teenager in a booth thanks you for stopping by then points at the gift shop. Inside are some cheap stickers, poorly made stuffed animals, and shirts. On a shelf, you learn the creature with six eyes is called Ortro and priced at nineteen ninety-nine as a black threaded ball with six felt dots stitched into it. The rest of the selection is equally disappointing, but your mother encourages you to pick something out.

"You want to remember today, right?"

You do. After all, it was a day spent with your mother. You pick out a t-shirt with "The Aquarium of Horror" printed on the front. The font choice is dull, and there are no pictures to add visual flair, but it fits over your white dress. A few months later, you'll lose the shirt and forget the name of the place as the memory nestles alongside forgotten dreams.

A few steps, and you're back on the hot pier. The air-conditioning had become so natural that you forgot how sweltering it is outside. To fight against the heat, your mother buys ice cream. The two of you sit on a bench as waves of people pass by. Some chocolate drips onto the shirt, but the dark blue fabric makes it impossible to notice.

The two of you chat about the aquarium, and she asks if you liked it. You said you did, and it's true. Listening, your mother nods. She asks what your favorite display was. You say the prophecy. The swirl of lights and the shadow of your future self still linger in the back of your mind. You hope to dream of it like you sometimes do of when your mother and father got along.

In fact, you will dream again of it. Much, much later, after the prophesized event had already occurred. You'll wake from the dream, covered in sweat as your own child lays nestled beside you. Memories of the aquarium will feel so clear you'd think you've read it in a story. The difference being, you finally understand the prophecy as if submerged in it like a sailor of olde.

The light tried to tell you of a disastrous family diner. Your mother will say something of your then dead father, and you'll explode on her. The first time in years. It will be an awful fight that ends in you fleeing with tears. On the drive back home, you'll think of your childhood because what else has your mother left you to think about? Intrusive thoughts will hit one after the other, and the small space of your car will start to suffocate.

You'll stop beside a random field, get out, and walk through it as if hoping to vanish into the distant tree line. Each step through overgrown grass will bring a new memory, and soon you'll traverse through the long history of quiet moments that made up your life. Not just the bad, but the good too. Like the day your mother took you to a random aquarium on the pier. You'll remember the shirt you lost, and feel a pang in your heart knowing it's gone forever.

In that field, you'll reflect, and it will be one of the most important moments of your life. It'll be when you accept how hard your childhood was for both you and your mother. You'll appreciate how much work your Granma put in to making a home, how tough the long hours had to have been for your mother who surely wanted to spend more days at piers with you, and how despite the massive love for your father, he was never a perfect man. That will also be when you allow yourself to hurt, to recognize the pain of wishing your mother had more to give, and that wishing for attention never made you selfish.

You will stand beneath a ghostly moon lurking in the shifting twilight, and despite the conflicting feelings of love and pain, you'll decide to forgive your mother. In forgiveness, you'll find a new, strange, horrifying, mesmerizing, beautiful peace you'll have never thought possible before.

But that moment is in the future. There is no forgiveness in you now because you're just beginning to recognize the pain.

As you two talk, the heat beats down on you. You watch the energy melt from your mother. You try to ask about her favorite part of the aquarium, but she gives vague answers. Some passersby step on her toes. Her face gets angry and red, blending with the sunburn set into her cheeks. Sweat soaks through the dress, making your new shirt heavy.

Your mother checks the time and accidentally lets out a sigh. You pretend not to notice, but your mother panics. She yanks you by the wrists to haul you to another attraction. Somewhere away from the heat and bitter guilt that swims behind both your heels.

Vast Enough To Swallow the Sky

~ *Michelle Muenzler*

The world was never so blessed as when my brother was born. At least that's what our mother always told us growing up, despite us being twins and looking near the same.

"More tea?" my brother asks, his hand sliding to the enameled pot he inherited from her recent death.

I blink, unable to speak. Speaking has been difficult since she died. Words so . . . lacking.

My brother's eyes are fever-bright as he tops off my tea, unconcerned by my lack of answer. "You've heard the news, yes?"

I nod, slowly.

"Good, good. It'll be a terrible storm," he says. "My first!"

I'm not sure what's so good about it. I glance outside the gardens of the estate—also his, thanks to our mother—and watch as green waves lap at the ancient seawall.

It's only with great struggle I find my voice. "The wall won't hold."

He laughs. "It will hold. It always has."

His confidence is maddening. Just like everything else about him. He's only a handful minutes older than me, but those few minutes are enough.

"It won't," I say again. Insistent that he listen.

But it doesn't matter what I say. He's my brother, the favored child and our mother's successor, and he's always done as he wills.

I remember the first time our mother let us watch a god-storm roll in. It crashed against the seawall, whipping strands of power in every direction.

"They're angry today," our mother said, and laughed. As if the anger of the gods was nothing but a trifle.

She held my brother by the hand, and my brother held me by mine, and my free hand squirmed, wishing for something of its own to grasp onto. Something to cling to and make sense of the cacophony of color and sound assaulting the air around us.

When our mother stepped onto the ancient platform that was her right—that great stone tongue jutting from the seawall to just above the raging waters—my brother quickly followed. I, on the other hand, balked.

Progress interrupted, our mother frowned. After a carefully considered moment, she nodded down at my brother and said, "Let him go. If your younger brother isn't brave enough to face the gods, he'll just have to stand with the rest of the powerless."

I like to think my brother paused before releasing my hand, but memory is a slippery serpent. What is real and what is remembered are not always the same thing.

I do know that I was left behind, though. Crying there on the beach behind the seawall until the villagers dragged me into their huddling mass to wait out our mother's miracle. And a miracle it was, like everything our mother did.

No godstorm ever survived her touch.

By morning, the skies have darkened to the color of peat, and rot stink rides heavy atop the heaving waves. The water is a brown churn, its bright green lost to the growing godstorm. It's difficult to breathe with the weight of the heavens pressed against my lungs. I don't think anyone has been struck by a godstorm this big in nearly a century.

My brother, however, doesn't cower. He stands midst the villagers at the lower seawall while hungry waves assault the barrier, intent on consuming the village and everything surrounding. Villagers touch my brother's robes. Whisper blessings as he passes. Next to them, the seawall shudders at the sea's wrath.

How like our mother he is in this moment. So bold, so sure of himself.

She would be proud.

The incessant knot in my chest burns, but I push my way through the crowds nonetheless and grab my brother's hand. "May you bring peace once more to the gods," I say, wind-swept grit scouring my face.

He pats me on the shoulder with his free hand. "Don't worry, I will."

I swallow my frown and instead inspect the adoration-filled faces surrounding him. Despite their watching eyes, I lean into him and whisper. "About the wall—"

He yanks me into a hug then, his mouth against my ear. "I said not to worry. Now hush before you ruin the big moment."

In his arms, with the entire village staring and the gods beating at our shore, I force a smile onto my face. "Of course. My apologies."

He slaps me on the back, then with a small shove returns me to the crowd.

A few moments later, storm winds lashing at his robe, he ascends the platform.

Nobody truly knows why godstorms form.

We speculate, of course, and pass down our speculations to the next generation. And over time, such things are considered lore, or truth. But what is truth? What could possibly be the meaning of such terrible storms?

I will tell you what they say.

The sea is a fragile vessel, like a ceramic cup. Fill it with enough anger, and eventually that anger must overflow, or else the cup crack.

And so the gods gather up all the hate and anger that has sunk into the depths, and when it becomes too much, they spin it into a godstorm that it might vent its rage elsewhere. That the cup may remain whole.

That elsewhere, of course, is us.

It's a pretty story, in its own way. Makes us feel like we're a part of the gods' plans. As though however overwhelming the storm, we have been gifted the power necessary to stand before it. Because what kind of gods would they be, otherwise?

What kind of gods indeed.

My brother stands on the stone platform, exposed to the waters whipping below. Rings of concentration spark around him as he attempts to harness the storm's frenzy and unravel it. Of all the people watching, though, only I can see his rings of power. Only I can feel the intense rage of the waters clutching at his feet, hungry to drag him into the godstorm's heart and drown the defiance from him.

I am my mother's child as well, after all. My blood as strong as his.

The sky howls as he starts funneling the storm's hatred away. I even begin to think that maybe I was wrong, maybe the seawall is not as weak as I feared. But then my brother pauses his work for the barest of moments. Turns his head toward me as if to say, *Do you see this? Is this not glorious?*

That moment of inattention is all the godstorm needs.

A fist-like wave pummels, not the platform upon which he stands, but the battered wall upon which it rests. And that is enough, for the seawall is indeed weak with age. Has grown weaker every storm.

The stones of the seawall crumple beneath him, and with it the platform he stands upon.

He wobbles a moment, his mouth a surprised 'o' and

the rings of his power flailing for purchase to keep him from plunging into the godstorm's wrath.

And then my brother is gone.

When our mother still lived, I used to dream of her death.

I pictured her, always at the lip of the storm, laughing at what the gods had flung in our direction. And while she laughed, I could feel the incoming waves, so intent on devouring her they shuddered through my bones. Such monstrosities, those waves. Vast enough to swallow the entire sky.

But it was only a dream. And no matter how many times I woke up screaming, our mother still stood against the next storm. And the next. And the next. Shaking her head in disappointment at my grasping hands, at my cracked voice begging her not to take those final steps up the platform.

And yet, in the end, it wasn't a storm that took her.

No, it was a bee. Minding its own business until the moment it wasn't.

She didn't know she was allergic until it stung her on the cheek.

And then . . . well, like so many moments in life, then it was too late.

☉

One moment, my brother is there. The next, he is gone.

Terrified villagers scream as waves spill through the seawall breach and snatch them toward the sea. So much screaming, and yet I can barely hear it past the ringing in my ears.

My brother . . . is gone.

A dozen hands shake at me. Thrust me forward, pull me back.

Someone yells, "Save us, damn you! Save us!"

And like that, my focus snaps into place.

The godstorm is terrible, the sky spitting in my face, the sea gnashing at my legs. Rage begets rage begets rage, the fetid mass of it geysering from the godstorm's heart. A rotting boulder of a storm, its ugliness crashing into the shore.

And yet, a thousand colors still split the air. Power lights up the sky in whipping strands.

My brother, trying to stop the storm even as it swallows him whole.

I thrust away the hands. The voices. Everything.

"Save yourselves," I snarl as the starving waves reach out once more for them. For me. And thrusting all my power forward like an arrow, I leap into the howling sea with but one purpose.

To take back my brother from its grasp.

I don't pretend to know the will of the gods.

Blessings and curses, trust and fate. Love and hate and fear and all the mess between.

It's the day before the godstorm still, and our tea is growing cold. And as my brother stares past the garden at the darkening sky, his hand trembles just a bit, dropping the ancient tea cup like bones against its saucer.

"Ah, damn," he says, staring at the cup. At the fresh spiderline crack snaking up its side. "I've broken it. Mother would kill me if she were still here . . ."

I nudge my cup in his direction. "Take mine", I say. "I never much liked tea anyway. Reminds me too much of the sea gone bad."

It's not until I notice him staring that I realize it's the most words I've strung together since our mother's death.

He accepts the cup with a slight nod, though. Returns to watching the sea. To watching the sky.

I, on the other hand, watch him. Try to remember that little boy who once held my hand, until the moment he did not. Try to discern if he is still in there, hiding somewhere beneath our mother's commands. Beneath her expectations. Or if we will forever be this—two brothers occupying the same space, together yet so terribly, terribly apart.

But all I can see are waves—those monstrous fists of the sea that have haunted my dreams for as long as I can remember. That haunt me now awake.

Rising, ever rising . . .

The Pack

~ Christi Nogle

I should never have let Lee move us out here. All that time we were hooked into Zillow, I secretly prayed she'd fixate on one with a smaller lot and higher square footage. Instead, we opted for acreage bordering public land, the house little more than an afterthought: one room for living, one for sleeping, one bathroom with the washer and dryer wrenched in, and a sloping lean-to added on to serve as workshop, guest room, storage for dog supplies and yes, kitchen. It was Lee's choice; I couldn't deny her.

Oh, but the outside made up for it those first few years. We were happy. Though there was nothing to see in town, Lee would drive in whenever we wanted and then, this: the thriving garden, the new puppy, the picnics and hikes. Lee trained all three dogs to be safe off-leash, which I'd never thought could happen. I planted flowers everywhere and trained morning glories, wisteria and orange-flowering trumpet vines up the walls to cover the ugly lean-to. We brought a tree guy out to prune the little orchard. The trees thanked us with so much fruit we had to take up canning.

Our bodies changed shape. We grew fatter from all the home cooking while our legs narrowed and toned from hiking and our arms grew brawny from woodcutting and gardening.

The truth was we both felt awfully fit up until Lee started getting the breaks. First was the fractured arm—a yellowjacket stung while she was high on a ladder picking apples. That one could have happened to anyone. It healed up right on schedule and then things just seemed to snowball: a fall on a hike and the ankle was screwed up, and it healed, and then a slip in the bathroom shattered her wrist, then the dogs didn't see Lee while they were running. She took a terrible crash to her ribs. We spent weeks in the city running up bills not just for the treatments and hospital room but also hotels, food, gas, dog boarding. Osteoporosis, the likely cause, was ruled out early. There didn't seem to be anything wrong with Lee's bones. What was making the accidents happen, then? It seemed like they investigated every little thing, her brain and inner ear to her toe-joints. In the end, all agreed that the series of breaks had been all coincidence.

Only now, between the lingering pain and the fear, Lee just about couldn't move. I didn't like to focus on it, but the bills would send me back to work. Not just a job (if indeed I could find one) but a commute. Little traffic, one would hope, but bad roads in the winter and deer shooting into the road.

The place was paid for, but I feared we'd lose it if the debt got too bad. Sometimes I felt we had already lost everything and just didn't know it yet. Other times I felt that fear was silly, something that could never happen, a sign of my losing it. We were both getting squirrely, but I tried to hide my own irrationality, tried to be strong for Lee.

Nothing got taken care of all that time. Vegetables froze in the garden, and with the thaw, the vines went wild. New ones with white-and-celadon blossoms joined and then overtook the rest. The trees went unpruned, fruit falling onto the ground, drawing wildlife, freezing and thawing to stink.

The dogs were distressed from being boarded and then neglected at home. I felt I didn't know these creatures who lost their cool chasing things off the property, sending me out into the forest with a flashlight, so helpless and small—scared of falling and breaking something myself, or being shot by a hunter. Even more, I feared that the dogs might be shot or break their legs.

I was always living through worst-case scenes, it seemed.

I hadn't been afraid of the woods with Lee, but it was different now. The first few times the dogs ran off in the night, I hyperventilated and bawled the whole time I searched. I resolved to chain them, which broke my heart all over again. They sat quietly indoors but would jump up and beg to go out whenever I made a move. They hated the chains but hated more to be inside with us.

Lee stayed in bed sweating and thrashing in terrible nightmares. I slept thinly on the bed's outer edge until Lee begged me to go elsewhere in case I might break her in my sleep. I carried my pillow into the lean-to and headed for the futon where we'd hoped some wandering relative or old friend might sleep one day. I stopped, gasped.

The vines had come inside the lean-to and made themselves at home, coiling around the futon frame, threading into the stove burners, groping into the bag of dog food with their spiny fingers. I'd heated up something or other on the stove not too long ago, so that infestation was new, but the other encroachments might not have been so new. Who'd been paying attention?

Lee hadn't come into this room in a while, either. I recalled that just the other day, she'd said she could not stand to be in the lean-to anymore. Maybe it was too cold?

Certainly drafts swirled in the room. The vines must have compromised the windows. I investigated. Yes, and they'd compromised the floor. The dog food was gone, and I had the strange thought that the vines had eaten it. Up close, their veiny green blossoms were formed like the propeller-seeds of maples—or like dragonfly wings. They had that pearly, iridescent sheen. Just now these blossoms riffled in the breeze inside the lean-to.

I stepped outside and hauled the dogs in by their chains. I stoked the fire, layered their beds and all the couch blankets onto the floor and set about bonding with them, stroking their fur and cooing to them. Dogs forgive. Soon we were a pack again, just the four of us. I regretted Lee being apart from this reconciliation, but I was weary. I coiled into the blankets, and we slept into the afternoon.

Lee, all this time, had one arm hanging off the side of the bed. Something hadn't healed just right, and it eased the pain to get some extra blood into her wrist. The whole arm dangled, tempting the new vines that were just then exploring that space between bed and wall. The vines reached out with grasping tendrils thick as fingers. Thinking of me, Lee held onto a wiry hand, squeezed it in sleep. The hand squeezed back. The hand raked through her sweaty hair on its way to her shoulder. It was afternoon, and my feet hit a creaky spot on the floor. Lee moaned, and the hand slipped back to its protected spot between the bed and wall.

"Dogs are out of food," I said from the bedroom doorway. I barely saw Lee in the darkened room and caught no hint of the vine. "I've got to go to town."

I didn't want to drive, didn't want to leave Lee.

"Can you get ginger ale?" she said.

I nodded. Yes, ginger ale, soup, and ice cream. All the foods for sick folks, though Lee wasn't sick. Just aching and scared. And heartsick, same as me.

It was sunny with scattered rain. The dogs enjoyed the ride. I did too. While we sped toward town, the vine repeated its travel up Lee's arm and through her hair, onto her shoulder, over her ribs. Only this time, Lee was awake and staring in awe. Lee's blood moved faster. Maybe the vine heard that or felt it. Felt it, most probably. A pulsing. The vine pulsed back.

While I trudged through the grocery store, the dogs were good. They paced, protecting the car, barking at shoppers who came close to the windows.

While they paced, the vine pushed against certain parts of Lee's body, the places where the breaks had been.

While I stood in the checkout line, a strange shiver went through me. *Lee—Lee's in danger.* Suddenly I needed to hurry home. I fumbled the change the cashier passed to me and left it scattered on the floor.

Another break, that's what I feared.

While the dogs pushed their noses out into speeding air, the vine began entry into the bone. Had it gotten a taste for marrow from the dog food? Or did it already know what it needed to form its fruit and its swarms?

This vine that had infiltrated so much else now plowed its slow way into its first human body. Not *victim*. No one thought of Lee as the victim, neither the vine nor Lee herself. This new thing she hadn't known to fear was come, and it was gentle. It burrowed deep and lay a seed into a crevice of unmended bone. Another seed, another.

While a Miata tailgated so hard I could barely breathe, the first seed sprouted—or egg hatched. It wasn't clear which. Lee felt a thrill. New layered blossoms like corsages opened rapidly from her wrist, from her ribs and leg and arm. She tore off her nightgown to see the wonder of them, celadon green but bordered in rose and gold and a hundred different blues, all rainbow-pearly as oil in puddles. They opened so powerfully that she heard another break. She felt nothing.

The convertible kept veering to pass and then tucking back in behind me. Now, finally, a stretch of empty road opened up. I slowed. The convertible came up alongside—

just as a truck entered the road. Someone lay on the horn and I veered, praying. *The dogs, oh, the dogs.*

But we were safe, all of us. We leveled out, slowed onto the shoulder. The red car was far in the distance now. I cried just briefly in relief, the dogs whimpering and licking my neck and face. Dogs have extra senses at times like this.

They felt it, saw it maybe: the anxiety that had held me so long was now dissipated.

While we had our moment on the shoulder, the blossoms grew larger. They grew firm with a lacy coral-like bone. Lee thought of flowers formed of porcelain. The vines that had held her retreated, making her slump and shatter in places. She felt nothing but was aware, watching. Her hand was farther from her body than it had ever been. The wrist was, it seemed, a deep pile of pollen—but animated. Crawling.

Lee was no longer the focus. Whatever happened, on and in her body, was beside the point. One sinewy vine lashed around her mouth, holding her fast to the bedframe, but the rest had moved on, lurking all around the bedroom door, just waiting for the four of us to walk into the room. Maybe the dogs were what it wanted all along, or maybe it would do something novel with my unbroken body. Lee would wait. She would see.

She would speak, soon enough. That last vine would loosen and move on to other entertainments. Later, as I dangled from the ceiling, as the dogs grew their beautiful, terrible wings, as the larval things filled up the air, we would be able to speak, to share notes. What had gone on while I was in town, what would happen next, what did it all mean, how would it end? There was no pain, and so what looked like destruction did not feel like destruction. It felt like a new beginning.

Yes, we would come back together, all five of us now, to share not regret but only wonder.

QUEEN of SWORDS.

On a Flayed Horse

~ Brandon H. Bell

Outside the window, San Muerte Drive glowed orange with dust kicked up by a band of flayed horses.

"Those creatures, they's part of the General's army. Trained to make conscripts. That means they kill folk," the crone said, huffing. "You see a load of conscripts passin', the horses ain't far behind."

"Everyone knows that," I said. The air in her shop stank of cigarettes and essential oils.

"Did you know they won't kill young women?"

I nodded, thinking of Muireann and Marigold. Thinking of my flight from him.

"The line between young and heart ripped out, who knows?"

She glanced at me and saw, I presumed, the disappointment and boredom.

"Did you know a young woman can ride a flayed horse?"
"Really?"

This was new and intrigued me.

"It'd be a bad idea," she said, cackles descending into wet cough.

In the distance black, shiny clouds roiled with faces and lightning. Tumblestorms. I wondered where the twins were, when they'd last eaten a hot meal, or when they'd last been hugged.

You might suppose my name is Chance. You'd be mistaken.

The last broadcast of import came from ground zero: it flooded social media, streaming, television. Everyone watched the descent, that sliver of ice in baby blue, suspended above Fort Worth, how it seemed to grow fatter, engorged, as it slid into place amid the meager downtown sprawl. Clips viewed more than any World Cup, Super Bowl, or Kardashian episode. The ship landed, and soon a crack of light at its base released its load and changed our world. The backs of people's heads filled the foreground. No holes bubbling with green alien spiders. Not yet.

After media died, our dim evenings echoed with snatches of voice and song from the Bardo, and I'd sit with her as long as I dared before bolting home in the night.

"You've met the General?"

She glanced at me; coughed her wet cough.

"Every Shaman has. You will too."

I remembered the old world, my parents, trips to the grocery store with dad and backyard hangouts while he grilled, constant chatter, laughter with mom, over what I couldn't recall, before I lived with *him*.

☉

I met Muireann and Marigold when I first arrived in the suburb from my uncle's home. Dust engulfed the sky, filtered maroon, crimson, and scarlet to a diffuse saffron horizon. Memory: firmament aflame, my hair mussed by the breeze, the dead equine reek. The twins, I learned, wandered the length of San Muerte when the hoards passed. They turned to me that day amid the band of flayed horses, first frightened at this haggard wraith, then chattering around meek, quick smiles. A tumblestorm wheeled past and they glanced for faces between lightning strikes. A children's game for the Bardo burbs. They creeped and charmed in equal measure, as the beasts herded around us. The destriers ripped men open and gulped out their hearts, a quick delicacy and a fresh conscript made.

They never bothered the twins.

Until one did.

A group of conscripts slouched through town, broken and bloodied by their harvesting band.

"You know why we treat women like we do, boy?" The old Shaman asked, laughing. Startled silent, she'd misgendered me.

Magic had rules, and she sought to share those rules before death came for her. Each step of our surest friend, as she dubbed it, counted in phlegmy, wet coughs, her every word a lesson meant to outpace the inevitable. From the window I watched the twins flit hand in hand across San Muerte, under red sky, silhouettes in dust. She cleared her throat, begging my attention, as she shared the secrets and rumors from the garrulous dead, stray artifacts, and the rare Bardonaut.

"I don't know how to answer a question that big," I said.

She laughed.

"Of course you don't. But know this. There's one way to bring someone back from the land of the dead. A fertile woman is needed. We all know it, instinctively. Gotta control a thing that powerful."

"Women ain't things," I said, feeling clever.

She laughed at that too, glanced with trepidation at the dim window behind her. Red sky and black expanse stretched to the horizon outside, but through that window sprawled a shadowed room beyond the building's perimeter, a room that shouldn't exist.

"Put that out ya mind," she said, noticing my attention. "Back to your litanies."

"It's like this in the dead land . . ." I intoned.

Inward, toward the landing site, the focal point in the war between humanity (dead and otherwise) and the aliens, life was brutal but quotidian. Severed limbs littered the ground, encampments congealed along the Trinity. Outward lay the Bardo, the dead land. Texas sprawled vast, black, and mythic beneath bloodshot sky. Wander too far out and you'd never find your way back. The dead, and other things, wandered inward, conscripts for the Buddhist General who led the dead army.

Winds carried hints of gunpowder and sewage, then weakened, stilled, and reversed, as if the city heaved a vast sigh, and from the Bardo the odor of lost dreams and forsaken love blew dust, ruffled hair, chapped skin.

The monsters, myths, and magic existed but slumbered, extraneous to the modern world . . . until the aliens arrived. They emerged from the Bardo, antibodies to a virus. The green pseudo spiders engorged people, sometimes other vessels (infamously Big Tex which roamed DFW, stalked the uninfected), and combined them into neomorphs. I'd crossed minotaurs, centaurs, and human centipedes on my trek from my uncle's.

In the suburb, we rarely saw neomorphs, but witnessed conscripts, determined for the front lines, and less often an Avicinaut, business suit aflame.

Once the green-pseudo-spider-filled Big Tex trudged into our suburb, then slinked to the water tower near Elm. There it stood, peering outward into the red and black, like a giant cartoon cowboy peering into all of human history. It latched onto the water tower like it would blow away and held vigil for three days. Near as I could tell, everyone stayed in their house, afraid to catch its attention.

Except the twins.

A band of horses arrived, following conscript. The girls trailed the horses to Elm, then stopped, gazed up into Big Tex's bland, bloated face. It tilted toward them, head askew like a mutt listening through a door. The girls waved at the monster.

It waved back, turned its face outward as if to take a last look, and then pivoted its significant bulk toward city center and set off into the fray, dripping green pseudo-spiders from its seams.

Later that day ten dark figures spilled from the Shaman's shop and trudged past my window, pale-faced and dour. No one had entered the shop since I left. I fidgeted and bit at my cuticles. Why did they come to her? They'd followed Big Tex, but where did they come from?

I berated myself, dismissed it, but a thought niggled at me. It was dark, square, foreboding.

A colossal migration inundated the town, and I sheltered in place, delinquent to the crone. I called her that, but she might have been forty. Rode hard and hung up wet, my uncle's East Texas twang intoned. He lived rent free and proffered these appraisals.

I once walked among the flayed horses, but she didn't know. Gave me a ring. *One ring to rule your ass*, she said, cackling. If I put it on backwards, her matching ring would spark: I'm coming, we agreed.

I strode once among the bands, when I was young, before I escaped my uncle's home, then as the means of my escape. Since then, I assumed a camouflage of ambiguity, let people assume. She'd assumed. Though I didn't saunter among the flayed beasts, it wasn't because of my gender, but my purity. I believed in my exile.

They accepted the twins. Sadness accumulated as I watched the horses and loved them from afar.

They'd crumpled my uncle like a plaything when I fled. Good horseys.

The knock startled me. I swung the door open and puzzled at the small, solitary figure against the dust haze.

Marigold threw herself into my arms, quaking. She smelled of wet puppies and bubble gum. I let her grieve for a moment, clutching at her like a lost doppelgänger, then I held her back and shook her. Her features hung on her face as if melted. Wounded by horror, the expression didn't register, and I stared into her eyes until the tiny rivulets on her cheeks, the quiver of her mouth, the fact of her solitude jolted me.

"Where is she?"

"A fffflayed horse," she whimpered. The world, and my stomach, churned.

The Shaman rarely left her shop, but the General would send a message to all the Shamans in a region and they'd travel to answer his summons at the foot of his tornado/tower.

On one such occasion, I broke into the shop and opened the black window. Cool breeze. Stink of gunpowder and must. I slunk through a series of rooms, a maze. The colors of the rooms: red-veined granite illuminated by cool light. I heard moans in a distant room, ecstasy or suffering, that morphed into indifference and grew sinister. I'd lost my way, forsaken the old stories. No trail of breadcrumbs, no diligently followed path.

Panicked, I stumbled into an alcove with a woman ensconced in a wooden chair. Ancient chicana, pale hair, wrinkled visage, cataract-filled eyes that flashed fear, then pity.

"Girl, you're not me, are you?" She asked, with kind inflection. She shifted, assessed this creature, and intelligence stormed in her cloudy eyes.

"I—I don't think so, ma'am."

"I was as young as you when it began. Old women are the ghostliest ghosts. What's your name?"

Not that much time had passed since ground zero. My brow furrowed. I told her my name.

"Not me. Why are you in the General's tower?" she asked.

I blanched.

She nodded, pushed up from her chair, trudged around the corner and led me to my window . . . the Shaman's window.

"Don't come back, girl."

I nodded on the windowsill to leave her.

"You knew I was a girl," I said.

"You'd of been killed or conscripted, otherwise."

☉

The tracks led into the red and black, through a valley of towering mesas straight out of a Chuck Jones cartoon. Not North Texas, at all. Mythic America. The tracks didn't resemble horse's hooves. Perfect circles, too small, damaged.

A zephyr ozone-sharp with perversion spilled from the Bardo; broken promise of rain dry enough to chafe. My lips puckered and cracked in a grit-filmed face.

"This is the one," I said to Marigold, and she nodded. The band surrounded us, stench and clouds of flies whipped by their sinewy tails. Innumerable rats followed the horses and Marigold violently kicked one that came near, an outburst, a fit. I paused and watched a mare prance alongside, muscles bulged, tendons tight, then released, blood black. I waited, breath held. It ignored me, kept the old unstated promise. It nickered and nodded, rolled eyes white with cataracts, then loped into grainy murk.

I squatted so I could stare, level, into Marigold's eyes. They were the clearest things I'd ever seen.

"Go to the Shaman. Tell her I've gone after Muireann. Tell her I'll use my ring. If she can bring us back—"

"I don't—"

"Just tell her, Marigold. Tell her I listened. Yes? But don't get too close. And then hide in the bands. Stay away from everyone. Watch the shop. That's where we'll come back. If we come back. It won't be long. If the General's tower moves and we haven't returned. Well, we probably won't."

Her face fell, stricken.

"A week?" she asked.

"At most. Yes. Be careful. Don't trust her. Don't trust anyone."

"I never did."

I rode into the Bardo on a flayed horse.

It's like this, in the dead land, I kept muttering. At my back ground zero, it's direction an extra sense, always apparent, a beacon, and ahead, infinite death, like a toothache.

Archetypal cacti caught grew in clusters, alongside more alien plants that resembled pairs of tall, cupped blades. Some were not plants, but the hunched profiles of deer-sized hares, towering ears a deadly mimicry.

When I passed, the king jacks—as I dubbed them— proved wary of my flayed horse but regarded me, salivating below impressive whiskers and quivering noses, their eyes blinking with lashes so lush they resembled fairy tale creatures until those mouths opened to reveal multiple rows of teeth.

Desert land, buttes, mesas, arroyos.

We crested a knoll above a river of the dead, flowing outward, a contemporary majority interspersed by the anachronistic, belonging to ancient eras. The dead slogged away from ground zero and toward the Bardo's horizon. The boundary throbbed, painful—outward endless death, inward the quotidian, opposing polarities that inspired nausea and weird gravity.

The horse trembled as we lingered atop the bluff, then we followed the trail of round tracks downward, into the dead masses' apprehension and furtive glances. The horse bucked, frustrated, eager to thrash, crush, bite and create conscripts. It tensed, adrenaline surged, a rumble began deep in its throat and I slapped its neck and told it *No!* The whinny sounded horror movie fake, and I slapped it again.

"No!"

Pointed our way and it clip-clopped on.

We parted the mass of bodies in our passage, none wishing to cross our path. The flayed horse eviscerated three stragglers that shuffled too near. They each fell to the ground with stillborn shrieks, but when I glanced over my shoulder, they rose and trudged against the flow, back toward the front. Even the dead could be conscripted. The horse seemed pleased and trotted, jaunty, through our parted red sea.

The tracks, like footprints of astronauts on the moon, undisturbed, led up the far grade. I hurried the skinless horse after them, and it obeyed as if it read my mind.

We came upon the linear city after crossing two more rivers of the dead. One river followed a ridgeline, the other trampled a sloped valley, crested accumulated skree, then emerged to flood the landscape. Cardinal directions ceased: there was inward, outward, and uncertainty. We cantered a Mobius strip trail, deeper into death. Titanic mesas predominated along a curvature no planet possessed, as the idea of direction grew alien, abstractions limited in my brain.

The tracks led down and into a house.

"Magic ain't nothing but shit you're too stupid to understand," the old woman said.

The memory lingered as I sat astride the flayed horse. What's the ish? The Shaman deemed it folly to ride a flayed horse. She tended to accuracy, bereft of details. Then I realized the problem.

I couldn't dismount.

Exploring the space between its hide and my pants, I found sinewy strands grew from its back into my buttocks and upper legs, joining us. It didn't hurt. In fact, if I strained just right, it felt . . . Exquisite.

Peered left, then right, atop a ridge a hundred meters above the line of houses, store fronts, municipal buildings. A ring. One side of the city faced inward toward ground zero, the other outward toward deep Bardo.

I could feel hunger from those depths as we poised above the gullet.

I paralleled the city, East then West (approximations), and found no end. If it went on, it would encircle DFW.

I could ride alongside it and I would come back to this spot. As I galloped, men came and went but ignored me.

Women slipped from the houses and shops, tended children, tossed out water, swept. Few acknowledged me, hands above scrunched faces.

All stood chained.

"Every town has a Shaman?"

The old crone nodded, smiled. My interest pleased her. We had the front door propped open, a rare luxury. No horses on San Muerte, nor Avicinauts nearby. Fresh air would be nice, she'd said.

"Do all the Shamans have a window like yours? The black one that leads somewhere else?"

She turned pale and fretted about the door, urged me to close it. She stood, faltered, collapsed in seizure, but recovered before I could react. I helped her up, trembling and sweaty, and led her to bed.

I returned to the tracks, indelible despite the wind, and followed them to the wooden boardwalk where they ended. The buildings had concrete foundations, and we sauntered, hooves high, to the near door, and the beast stomped—

Jigsaw splinters, slap of board against concrete, into the hovel where Muireann lay chained. Two men, Caucasian but dark with hair, beard, aura, stood above her. To the side lay a contraption that resembled a horse-shaped cab for two and supplies above spindly legs driven by pedals.

"You cain't—" one man said before the destrier tensed, reared, then clomped, its shriek loud, horrible in the lamplight of the small abode. It took care not to stomp Muireann, unconcerned about the particulates and spatters of blood. She closed her eyes but did not scream. She'd walked among the horses and understood their alignment.

When the room fell to a quiet composed of the flayed horses' breath and whinnies, clomping of concrete, she slipped from her shackles, and stood, wiping hair from her face. I searched, found a jacket hanging, and laid it over the horse. Then I leaned down and snagged Muireann beneath thin arms and plopped her astride the cloth.

"Chains didn't stop you," I said.

"They said I'd grow into them."

Nothing to lose but our chains . . . the thought blazed in my mind, lit my eyes, burned at my skandhas.

The woman next door toppled from the boardwalk, chain pulled taut. Neighbors yelped, afraid, or sniped in rage, flashing eyes and waggled fingers. The horse had its way with them, Muireann quiet but trembling, and a dozen conscripts rose from the blood and viscera of their protestations to shuffle toward the front.

I urged the horse further along the inward boardwalk of the city, far enough that they would not have been able to hear the death stomps and screaming from earlier.

We arrived at a storefront with a cheerily painted sign. Odds N Ends. The name seemed ominous. A woman stepped onto the boardwalk in response to my knocking. She wore a simple shift, smiled.

"Hola, mi ja. Can I help you?"

A shackle and chain around her ankle.

"I've come," I said. Muireann glanced back and up at me. "We've come to rescue you."

"From what, mi ja?"

"You're chained. A prisoner. We—"

I didn't know what to call it. This gate in our wombs. This resource everyone but us might control.

"Ah, mi ja, so it goes. This is life, yes?"

She smiled.

"I miss Marigold," Muireann told me.

"I know. Soon," I said.

From home to home, shop to shop, we searched. I spoke to the women who would listen. Countless men fell beneath my hooves. I could have counted, but grew numb to gore and screaming.

We traveled the length of the linear city. The ebb and flow of death beckoned, urging toward the Bardo depths, endless death, a promise, a withheld caress.

I'd been right. The linear city stretched around all of DFW.

And I was wrong on all points that mattered.

"I miss my sister," she reminded me.

"I know. Let's go."

I flipped the ring on my finger. It glowed blue, as if in a book of stories and ogres were near.

"Your surest friend knocks, lady," I said aloud. I didn't know if the magic conducted my voice, but I thought it fair to give her the chance to refuse this if it did. Static suffused the air along with the scents of offal and iron.

The flayed horse started, then bucked and trotted off into the badlands. Sky dark red, black expanse, until the flash of light and cracking, sand in eyes, then blood, an infinite vortex of suffering and shock—

I recognized her screams—

The emergence, like birth. Stifling air, gloom. Tunnel's end, a dead scream echoed. The walls speckled with viscera and blood. Heaving breath, still alive, then awareness, the tick, tick, tick of time. The tiny figure in the corner, peering at her sister. Bawling for her sister.

"Go," I say, and leverage Muireann down. She topples to the floor, then scampers into an embrace with her twin. Marigold breaks free and scampers near, balled fist lifted toward me, eyes intent. I reach down and she slips something small, cold, and round into my palm. Then she runs back and they hold each other, eyes closed.

The moment elongates, their embrace, their scurried escape, open door blinding, but their passage dims it and they slink into a passing band. He clears his throat and I notice the figure. Doesn't look like a monk. Business suit over enormous girth, orange tan, blond hair, dead eyes.

"You look like that president," I say and he laughs.

"I wonder," he tells me. "Why you have killed one of my Shaman? Your mentor, no less?"

His voice is curt, formal, sensual. He doesn't look like a General, either.

"The linear city, those women. Why?"

"Linear city? The Bardo gives us interesting perspectives, yes? I'd call it a circular city. Huge. It's the hugest."

I take a moment to understand the sound chuffing from his face is laughter.

"Are you a monster?"

At this he mewls, the amusement settling into ugly gentleness.

"Hard question, Shaman killer. I am Rakshasa, bitten by Cucui," He says and laughs again, entertained, "all those years ago. They called me, in time, Geshe Rakshasa. More recent: General."

"I mean. Did you have all those women chained? In the city?"

"Interesting thing, the Bardo. We're told by mendicants it's an in-between place. But you see, it is a form unto itself, a function, a mode, a multifarious proliferation thereof. And it has interesting ways of formalizing the circumstantial, actualizing the memetic. Big words. It gives you what you really are. I make use of that, fighting the incursion—"

I rear the horse and turn to the window. The rakshasa in his fine suit hisses at my back as we burst through the glass and into his tower.

The thing I understand about magic? Understanding is overrated.

Three days pass, measured in glimpses of sky from occasional parapets, machicolations, balastraria, windows. The aether is thick and Bardo radio waves provide esoteric nomenclature—fun, I guess—but most useful, often betrays nearby pursuers, minds static with bloodlust. The General's elite guard follows, soldiers more skilled and quiet of mind, but I've outpaced them and their insectile-buzz auras, the tower Tardis-vast.

A psychic confluence grows stronger, up feels like outward, the Bardo twisted tight. I gallop along black basalt corridors wrapped within this coil of space-time, up the superstring.

Where did I hear that phrase?

I wonder about the relationship of tower to Bardo, but that's another useless question I'm too stupid to answer.

The elite guard in pursuit, I meet iterative versions of the old woman I encountered in the black window.

I speak with these doppelgangers—each time, first contact—wondering how to entreat them to my cause. It is her hand I ask for, to hold in momentary kinship, and it is her ring that intrigues me.

Were but she of child-bearing age.

That is interesting, I think from within the flayed horse's skull. I agree, the thought unfurling in my girl's brainpan. As I travel up the spire, the iterations of the elderly woman become younger—merely old, next middle-aged, then younger still . . .

Crack, crack, crack—

The woman crumples with a whimper. Quiet flutter of breath. The echo lives longer than she does and the bullet hole drools onto her hair and the stone floor, then the next report and a punch at my flank. The horse parts of me are magic-dead, but it still hurts like hell.

Canter into shadowed lee, break into gallop, follow an upward path around an outward wall, the tower smells of mold and agelessness, light filtered through rare balastraria give false impressions of cold mountains and forests just beyond the next corner. Damp, refreshing, breath heaved in cold, but steaming on the exhalation, the running warms, and adrenaline makes me eager and jumpy. The squad proves persistent, fast and pursuit remains intense and threatening. Gunshots dull my hearing.

Pass into a region of the tower composed of large chambers shaped like the inside of a nautilus shell, cathedrals within cathedrals turning into profane fleshy limbs, entwined.

Charge ever upward. Magic-dead, I never tire, onward, upward, mindless, until unknowable kotis of kalpas of space-time elapse and . . . I come upon this girl, almost a child. She shrinks back, a ghost. But we see each other and linger on the exposed topmost parapet of the tower. She cries, eyes the horse—aware, it seems, of the danger of flayed horses but not of their embargo toward young women—overcomes her fear—

Far below stretches the battle-torn landscape of DFW. Beyond that, the red and black of the Bardo, mesas, endlessness.

"He tricked me. Everyone thinks—"

"The General," I say.

Confusion mars her face. The wind smells of rain—such beauty—and a hint of blue flashes between gray clouds.

"The old monk," I say.

She nods.

"You think a ring holds all the world's magic, someone once told me, but on a woman's finger, it's a gate. You've bled?"

Confusion again, but a meaningful glance clarifies and she nods.

"We could destroy this, but you'd be a gate. And that means—"

"I'm a ghost. You don't know what it means."

I slip the Shaman ring Marigold gave me onto her finger. I nod at it and she wrenches the apprentice ring from her finger and slips it on mine.

"You know how the old magic works?"

She shrugs.

"It's dangerous. To your shaman, to you."

"I consent," she says. "I take responsibility."

She doesn't grasp the breadth of what's been done to her, iterative hell of so many lost selves growing old, alone, trapped. But no sense in adding to her misery.

I take the girl's apprentice ring, flip it and slide it back onto my finger. It glows blue.

The girl's corporeal self wears the apprentice ring, the original, suspended in an upside-down car, wreckage imminent. A magic I do not know holds this pocket of space-time. Another ghost version of her stands beside me, observes me, observes herself and her family in the moments before impending death.

"He did this to me. To us. I don't understand why."

"Why never really matters," I say.

She's startled at my reply. Cries. Since the beginning, no one has heard her.

"Please," she says. Through tears, she begs for the Shaman's ring.

I re-enter the dark, fetid temple to parse through the explosion of flesh within.

The Shaman's remains cool in the pizzeria-turned-temple. I locate her hand and retrieve the ring. I wipe the effluvia, blood, and gore from it and shamble out to the floating Subaru. Through the open window I place the Shaman ring on the girl's finger. I pretend it a gift from me to her, a promise, a vow composed of secrets and silences only we might decipher.

It is like this in the world. Soldiers fight, civilians shelter, evils parade in daylight, men-shaped creatures, everywhere, and those not conforming to these man-shapes are murdered, maimed, or raped out of hunger, power, boredom; why doesn't matter. Those with uteruses get pregnant, give birth and raise the seeds of violence, perpetuating the cycle. Men-shaped creatures with holes in the back of their heads bubbling with green pseudo-spiders battle the General's army; other-than-men lay dead or dying, limping from trespass to desecration, conscripts incoming, another band of flayed horses, glory, glory, hallelujah.

Engorged, still my dual, eldritch self, flayed horse from the Bardo and battered babe from the battlefields of suburbia—Ha!—but more still: filled with the green pseudo-spiders and crouched on the giant's shoulder as I flip the ghost girl's ring to return.

The old magic is mine.

Stark horizon where bruised sky paints the world in chiaroscuro, a front of tumblestorms blow inward, their shadows like fingers in a nightmare. Time slows, an artifact of the superstring or I'm clogged with adrenaline.

It's like this in the dead land: on a flayed horse I fall toward the tower, head full of green alien spiders. They bubble in my craniums, horse and human, multifoliate chimera. I fall past Big Tex, it, too, emergent from the ghost girl's womb, and she hovers near, correct that this is magic. Shit I don't understand.

We plummet, Big Tex, ghost girl, and I toward the tower. The soldiers in black and their General wait, but even now iterative ghosts of her fall into her more corporeal selves, alight with rage. We use his magic against him, her iterations become an army to defeat this last vile patriarchy.

You might suppose my name is Chance, but you'd be wrong. It's Necessity.

PAGE of PENTACLES.

Charlie Eats the Paper Gods

~ H. L. Fullerton

Nothing at FAIHT (Featherstone's All Inclusive Harmonic Tutelage—the most-exclusive, inclusive, learning-centric kindergarten preparatory) was ever considered a problem. Until four-year-old Rederick Thuman joined Miss Kinders' class.

"How did you do that?" Tommy Yen-Zarif whispered across the snack table to Rederick.

"I didn't do it," Rederick said. "Charlie did."

"What else can Charlie do?" Evergreen Masoda asked. "Can he make my milk chocolate?"

"Charlie can do anything."

"My milk's still white."

Rederick shook his head the way his mom did when he forgot to put the toilet seat down. "That's 'cause you don't believe."

"I believe," Tommy said and Tommy's milk turned colors.

"Charlie likes you now," Rederick said and hummed while he ate the rest of his jelly and cream cheese sandwich. Miss Kinders, who was eavesdropping on the exchange, turned white and clutched the pentagram she wore around her neck.

☉

When Miss Kinders (whom Mrs. Featherstone had hired as much for her fantastic name as her qualifications) first mentioned the Rederick-Charlie situation, Mrs. Featherstone thought she'd have to fire Miss Kinders for being intoxicated. Then Mrs. F herself witnessed Rederick's . . . well, it could only be called indecency, and decided a sip, or a fifth, of vodka was in order before inviting Rederick's parents in for a chat about the Disappearing Paper Dolls.

Mundie Thuman, Rederick's mother, texted her husband during her phone conversation with Mrs. Featherstone's assistant, first to determine his availability for their meeting with the headmaster, then to theorize what the agenda would be and how they should handle things. Both agreed that no matter what the infraction was and it had to be an infraction, right? No one was summoned into the headmaster's office as a reward and Eamonn assured his wife that he'd sent in the tuition money so it wasn't anything financial . . . Yes, yes, tuition had most certainly been paid; he was looking at confirmation from their bank this very second. Puzzled, the Thumans agreed that whatever this was about, they would take Rederick's side because children needed to know they were loved unconditionally. Any punishment, if warranted—oh, what could Red have done?—would be handled at home. By them. The Thumans parenting style could best be described as 'United Front' and this was what they presented to Mrs. Featherstone.

First thing Mrs. Featherstone—who'd taught the pre-K set for three decades and had dealt with all sorts of delicate issues—asked the Thumans was, "Have either of you taught Rederick magic tricks?"

"Magic?" Eamonn said, at the same time his wife said, "No."

The headmaster made a check mark on the papers in front of her. "Ventriloquism?"

The Thumans shook their heads.

"And you're still practicing humanists?"

"Perhaps," Mundie said, feeling in control for the first time since she'd entered the building, "you best tell us what this is about."

Mrs. Featherstone sighed. "Rederick's pranks are disrupting the class. We understand the enthusiasm of young minds, encourage it at its proper time and place, but Rederick's in—" Here Mrs. F. almost blurted 'indecency', but caught herself at the first syllable, "*enthusiasm* is affecting the other children's ability to learn."

"What kind of pranks?" Eamonn asked. He was careful to modulate his tone, keep any pride out of it, but he couldn't help thinking, *My Red's an entertainer.* Still, the boy Mrs. Featherstone was describing didn't sound like their Rederick. Eamonn had to work to get his son to smile, such a serious boy he was; him clowning about in class was hard to imagine.

"Miss Kinders had the class cut out paper dolls. It not only allows them to practice fine motor skills, but illustrates how we are all connected and depend on one another. Also, it encourages them to stay in line and hold hands whenever we leave the classroom. A strong chain will never lose a link, I always say."

"What does this have to do with Rederick?" Mundie asked. She glanced at her watch to remind Mrs. Featherstone how important the Thumans' time was, how expensive. "Did he refuse the assignment?"

"No, no. Rederick participated. But after . . . well, some of the chains disappeared."

Mundie straightened in her chair. "Are you accusing our son of *stealing* other children's *paper*?"

"Not stealing." Mrs. Featherstone pursed her lips. "Some of the children encouraged Rederick to . . . show off. I, myself was there. He said, 'Eat the dolls' and then the dolls disappeared. Like a magic trick."

Eamonn, a jokester himself, said, "Did you check his sleeves?" His wife frowned her eyes at him and his smile disappeared.

"We checked everywhere for the dolls and couldn't find them." Mrs. Featherstone didn't mention that it had, in fact, looked like someone was dining on doll spaghetti. Chains of paper dancing in the air, then disappearing into an unseen gullet. Chimp, chomp, gulp and little confetti flakes falling to the floor. No, no need to mention that to the Thumans. They'd think she'd gone 'round the bend. As it was, they looked at her as if she were the

Big Bad Wolf and they a couple of woodcutters with new hatchets.

"Did you ask Rederick about the dolls?" the mother said.

"He blamed it on Charlie."

"Have you spoken to this Charlie's parents?" the father asked.

"There is no Charlie," Mrs. Featherstone said, then, "There's more." And she told the Thumans about how it rained glitter during quiet time; the banana stickers on the ceiling; the marbled crayons which made it impossible to teach children their colors, the re-arrangement of the alphabet letters; the now-you-see-it-now-you-don't missing keyboards, Rederick's insistence on Charlie as the perpetrator of all these acts and the way he'd convinced the other children to believe in—and blame—his imaginary friend. Then she mentioned the disappearing paper dolls again because of its leap from harmless-but-concerning behavior to something that needed to be dealt with immediately. "We'd like to work on helping Rederick discern real and imaginary and hope that you can reinforce that distinction at home. Reinforcement is very important at this age, as I'm sure you know. It's one of FAIHT's four columns of learning. Perhaps the most important." Mrs. Featherstone folded her hands across her desk, partly to keep the trembling hidden, but also to impress upon the Thumans that if they didn't stop this Charlie business, she'd have no option but to expel Rederick. By the looks on their faces, the Thumans understood her unspoken threat.

☉

That evening at the dinner table, Eamonn and Mundie exchanged looks over Red's head, wanting to approach the subject of Charlie in the best manner possible. At no point should Red feel as if they were accusing him of anything. They would simply ask him about Charlie, then decide if they needed to make an appointment with a child psychologist. Perhaps their pediatrician could prescribe something. Most likely Mrs. Featherstone and Miss Kinders were wrong about Charlie belonging to Red's imagination. Red would tell them it was someone's nickname or another child's creation and they'd all breathe easier, maybe even laugh.

"I'm done," Rederick said. "Can I color?"

"May I," Mundie said and Red shimmied off his chair until his toes touched the floor, then went running for paper and crayons. The Thumans eyed the crayons, happy to see they were all solid colors— just the way the manufacturer sold them. It gave their faith a boost: all would be okay.

"Hey, bud," Eamonn said, picking up a crayon. "Tell us about Charlie."

"Charlie's silly." Rederick drew a sun, colored it purple.

"Have we met Charlie?" Mundie said.

Rederick shook his head. "You can't see Charlie."

"Because we're grown-ups?"

"No. 'Cause Charlie's imaginary. Like the wind."

Both Thuman parents inhaled sharply. Mundie urged her husband to 'go on, ask' so he said, "Wind is a real thing. Did you mean imaginary as in something that's made up, like you made Charlie up, or invisible as in something you can't see with your eyes?"

"Charlie's invisible."

The Thumans sat back in their chairs. This wasn't going according to plan. Mundie braved, "Is Charlie a friend? From school?"

Rederick tilted his head as if considering the question *or listening.* "He says he is."

Eamonn looked at Mundie. She looked at Rederick, mouth tight. "Did you read about Charlie in a book?"

Their son stopped coloring and giggled. "You're silly. Charlie's not in a book. Kids can't read. Charlie's in the sky. Is the sky invisible or imaginary?"

The Thumans could see their approach wasn't working. Red wasn't about to confess to making up a prankster persona. Eamonn decided to dig deep and coach the answer out of his son. There had to be a reason Red was pretending about Charlie and if they could figure out what that was, then they could cure their son and he'd turn into a happy, well-adjusted pre-schooler with a bright education ahead of him. It took a few tries to pry Red's attention off the sky's realness. Eamonn wanted to take the crayons and paper away from his son—but that's what his father would've done so he knew it wasn't the right thing to do. "Mrs. Featherstone told us about the paper dolls, son. You know it isn't right to rip up other kid's work. It might hurt their feelings. You wouldn't want anyone to rip up your drawing, would you?"

Red looked at his dad. "You're gonna rip up my drawing?"

"I'm not going to do anything to your drawing. I just want you to understand that you have to be respectful of people's things. I know you know how to share. Well, sometimes sharing means not touching or breaking other people's things."

"Okay."

"So you won't make anything else disappear like the paper dolls, right?"

"It wasn't me. It was Charlie."

The Thumans felt like failures. Their son wasn't understanding them at all. Did he know what an expulsion from FAIHT would mean on his permanent record? Why was this happening to them? Eamonn tried one more time. "Why would Charlie do something like that, Red?"

"Pommer said he wouldn't believe in Charlie unless Charlie ate the paper dolls so Charlie ate them."

"Rederick. Charlie isn't real." Mundie put her hand over her son's drawing. "He's imaginary. Like the cartoons you sometimes watch on TV."

"No. Charlie's real. He's a god. Like Evergreen's Yahweh and Pommer's Vishnu and Miss Kinders' Crone and Green Jesus."

"But, Red, honey," Mundie said, using her best child-friendly voice, which was the same sing-song manner she used at work for stupid employees, "we're humanists. We don't believe in gods."

"I believe in Charlie." Rederick took his crayons and went to his room. Eamonn and Mundie stared at each other, each hoping the other knew what to do next. None of the parenting articles they'd read said anything about what to do if your child created his own god.

"It's all-inclusive," Mundie said when her husband balked at her strategy for handling Mrs. Featherstone. "It's right there in the name: Featherstone's *All Inclusive* Harmonic Tutelage."

"I don't think we should encourage this 'god' thing."

"We're not encouraging. This is just a phase. It'll pass. Three months from now Red won't even remember making Charlie up. But do you want Red kicked out of kindergarten prep over an imaginary friend who thinks eating paper is the height of comedy? Do you want his future ruined?" Mundie stared at Eamonn until he answered.

"No."

"Then we tell Mrs. Reinforcement-is-one-of-the-four-pillars-of-enlightenment what Red told us: Charlie's his god. All faiths, creeds, whathaveyou are welcome at FAIHT. Well, Red's now a Charliest. I've already filled out the declaration form and you'll drop it off when you take Red to school."

"You didn't actually put 'Charliest,' did you?" Eamonn said.

"Don't be ridiculous. There isn't a box for that. I checked 'monotheist, other'. Thankfully, Rederick hasn't created an entire pantheon so we only have to get rid of one god. How hard can that be? In the meantime, if that woman tries booting us from her school, we'll sue for religious discrimination."

"I don't think—"

"Eamonn. We. Are. Doing. This."

Eamonn dropped the paper off. He also explained to Rederick about the imaginary nature of gods and that Charlie was only an attempt to make sense of a world that Red didn't quite understand, but one day Red would learn physics and then he'd see there wasn't anything to be afraid of and there was no need to believe in a larger power directing unseen forces. Red said, "I'm not afraid of Charlie, Daddy. He makes me laugh." and ran down the hall. Then he ran back. "Here. Charlie made this for you. You can use it at work." Rederick handed Eamonn an orange crayon containing squiggles of blue, green, brown and pink. It still had the maker's paper label tightly wrapped around it. Eamonn rolled it between his fingers until he could read the color's name: Atomic Tangerine.

He clutched his present and wondered if it was possible for a four year old to use crayons as a foreshadowing device.

Miss Kinders stared at the form on her desk and realized that the Thumans knew nothing about religion; otherwise they'd never have declared Charlie a god. In front of her, the class whispered about Charlie in that stage-whisper way small children had—not a true whisper, more of a sibilant yell. She had to get the class under control, get Charlie under control. A magical imaginary friend was bad enough, but now with half the class professing faith in 'Charlie' and the Thumans declaring his godhood . . . Miss Kinders stood. Her chair scraped against the floor and the children laughed.

"Charlie made the chair fart," Pommer said.

Contradicting children only made them argumentative so Miss Kinders dragged a screeching marker across the white board and regretted that chalkboards went the way of pen and paper—fingernails across a chalkboard would've made a much more satisfying sound. "I make the things in my classroom . . . talk." Miss Kinders pulled her authoritative voice out of her bag of tricks. "I also make them quiet and that includes all of you. There will be no art today. Instead, we're going to talk about gods." Murmurs broke out. Eyes glanced Rederick's way. Miss Kinders rapped on her desk, feeling a bit like Poe's raven. "And rules. We'll talk about gods and rules."

Rederick's face bunched up. He crossed chubby arms across his tiny stubborn chest. "Gods don't have rules."

"Yes," Miss Kinders said. "Yes, they do. Let's start with the ancient gods. Anyone here worship Zeus or Apollo?" Two hands went up. Miss Kinders let out the breath she'd been holding. Her double minor in comparative religion was about to make itself useful. If she couldn't make Charlie disappear, she'd truss him up with restrictions so tight he'd wish he were imaginary. It never occurred to her that she herself had made the mistake of believing in him.

☉

On his way to work, Eamonn worried that he and Mundie were committing a monumental parenting blunder, the kind other parents would whisper about and shake their heads until someone said, "Well, it's not surprising about the Thuman kid. Remember how he invented a god and his parents declared it a religion? I mean, you might expect something like that from animists, but a couple of atheists should've known better." Expulsion was the least of their worries; Red could be socially ostracized. His friends' parents would never invite over a kid who came with his own god and a boatload of glitter. The Thumans didn't have the social or financial clout to pull a thing like that off. Maybe Mrs. Featherstone had done them a favor by threatening expulsion. This way they could nip this Charlie thing in the bud before it did more than smudge Red's future. Next year Mrs. Featherstone would be a memory in a scrapbook; it was the other pre-K thru 12 parents he and Mundie needed to keep ignorant of the Charlie situation. He'd message her as soon as he reached the office so they could strategize.

Mrs. Featherstone was on the phone with the Yen-Zarifs who were concerned that their son Tommy was being recruited by a cult. They wanted to know if 'All Inclusive' meant that proselytizing was condoned on campus. They wanted it stopped. They wanted Tommy switched to another class and kept away from this Charlie and his religious ramblings, and they wanted contact information for Charlie's parents. What kind of people let their child believe that God spent his time turning white milk into chocolate? The Yen-Zarifs were all for religious tolerance, but this type of talk was sacrilegious. And, they reminded her, Tommy was not supposed have chocolate—it contained caffeine and the Yen-Zarifs' religion prohibited caffeine. Also, potassium sorbate made Tommy unruly.

"Mr. and Mrs. Yen-Zarif, I fully understand all your concerns and, of course, we have Tommy's dietary—" Here, Mrs. Featherstone remembered not to use the word 'restrictions' because parents who sent their children to Featherstone's All Inclusive Harmonic Tutelage did not want any reminders, even subliminal ones, that their progeny were prevented from participating in anything, even those things they themselves had expressly forbidden. The role of FAIHT was to open doors, not slam them shut and engage the deadbolt. "—*requirements* in his file. Please be assured that FAIHT was unaware that food sharing was occurring. I will make sure that stops today. I cannot, however, due to legal ramifications, release information on other children or their parents. But I will see about relocating Tommy to an environment better suited to his needs. While diversity is one of FAIHT's four columns of learning, we can't allow it to negatively affect any of our students." She'd also see about getting Rederick Thuman under control. If Miss Kinders hadn't any success in curbing the boy's imagination, then perhaps she wasn't the wunder-lehrer Mrs. Featherstone had imagined.

Miss Kinders marched her class through the halls to the library. "No whispering," she said, keeping her eyes straight ahead so she couldn't see any more things that would shake her faith. She was adult. She knew better. She'd show Red books filled with commandments; she'd show him that you couldn't just invent a god and let it do whatever it wanted; she'd show him; she'd show them all.

At his desk, Eamonn Thuman reached for a pen and picked up the many colored crayon. How strange the crayon felt in his hand, not like a pen at all, but something mightier. Would it work?

Eamonn pulled a blank sheet of paper from his printer and scribbled circles on it. The crayon worked. That surprised him though he wasn't sure why. Then he caught sight of his scribblings. It was if . . . It looked like . . . but it couldn't be . . . Eamonn shaded another section of paper and yes, an image was appearing. The crayon was functioning like his printer, except instead of laying down black letters on white paper, it was creating a waxy painting *without being told to.*

He adjusted his grip. Realized that the wrapper was now pink. He checked its name. Atomic Tangerine had morphed into Radical Red. Heart jumping in his chest, Eamonn put the crayon tip to paper and colored. When he'd filled the page, he saw Red and a bunch of other kids running around tables piled with books. A woman towered over them, her eyes raised to the heavens, her face twisted in a scream, her arms clawing at air.

Eamonn shook his head, but the picture didn't disappear. He flipped the page and threw the crayon onto the floor. He focused on his computer screen and willed himself to forget what just happened. But he couldn't. He kept thinking, *Charlie*. His eyes drifted towards his desk and the overturned paper. Which wasn't blank. It was the declaration form he'd handed to Miss Kinders. Stomach sinking, he picked up the form and peeked at the back. The drawing was still there, and maybe, just maybe, the figures had moved. Eamonn squeezed the form.

Miss Kinders. Eamonn scrambled from his desk, form in hand, and grabbed the crayon off the floor. He headed back to FAIHT.

Streamers of paper-god cut-outs flew from FAIHT's collection of holy tomes, decorating the library as if it were a non-denominational pine tree. Kids clapped and twirled, laughed and chased the paper gods. Miss Kinders shouted for them to sit down and be quiet. She grabbed at books only to have them torn from her hands.

"Noah's ark!" Evergreen Masoda pointed to the train of paper animals dancing across the shelf tops.

"Look, it's Vishnu," Pommer said, eyes wide as his god's form emerged from the pages of a book, arm in arm in arm in arm.

A string of pentagrams, like the one around Miss Kinders' neck, twined around her, pulled her into a waltz. She broke free. "Enough," she yelled. Her eyes locked on Rederick and she marched towards him. "You stop this now. There are rules. I showed you the rules. *You have to follow the rules.*"

"Charlie doesn't like rules," Rederick said, eyes focused somewhere high above her left shoulder. "And Charlie isn't in a book. Gods shouldn't be in books. Gods can't write."

"The goddess—"

Rederick interrupted her. "Charlie says he can eat all your gods."

Miss Kinders stepped back from Rederick, mouth open, hand clasped around her necklace. "No," she said, but already pages of god-dolls were disappearing. Motes of paper fell to the floor, coating everything in a grayish dust. "No!" she screamed.

"You can't trap gods in books," Rederick said. "Rules make them weak."

"There is no Charlie," Miss Kinders said. "It's you. And I can stop you." Courage gathered, she ran at Rederick.

The library door crashed against the wall, but Miss Kinders wouldn't be distracted, so she didn't see Rederick's father race into the library, waving a piece of paper. He stopped short when he realized the teacher was lunging at his son. Tables, chairs and children separated him and Rederick. Eamonn couldn't get to her before she got to Red. Not knowing what else to do, he threw the crayon Charlie made for him at Miss Kinders.

It hit her in the head. There was a soft pop. A cloud of glitter exploded into the room and everything froze. Rederick moved out of reach. Said, "I'm okay now." and everyone unfroze.

Miss Kinders' pentagram rose towards the ceiling. Her arm yanked at it, but it kept rising, pulling her to her toes. Her fingers burned and she let go. Watched as her encircled five-sided star was crushed into a 'C' and dropped against her chest. The fight went out of her then. She slumped in a nearby chair, one meant for a body much smaller than hers, and wept.

"Did you see her necklace?" Tommy said. "C is for Charlie." The children stopped frolicking and gathered around her in a circle. "Tell us another story about Charlie," they said and sat at her feet.

Eamonn Thuman grabbed his son and headed for the nearest exit. He slowed when he realized Red had grabbed another boy's hand and that boy was holding the hand of a girl in a green dress and Eamonn realized he'd turned into the Pied Piper leading a line of children into the hall. He set Red down, found his son's hand, and said, "Okay, we're all going to go see Mrs. Featherstone and give Miss Kinders a moment to herself." He tried not to think about reappearing declaration forms, exploding glitter crayons, or how much he and the children looked like a chain of paper dolls.

☉

The Thumans withdrew Rederick from school that very afternoon and sued FAIHT. Miss Kinders was fired for proselytizing to her students and instigating the kiddie faith riot, which is what the media dubbed the library incident. Mrs. Featherstone decided inclusiveness was more trouble than it was worth and renamed her kindergarten preparatory the Fourth Academy for Cooperative Thought, or FACT.

Rederick didn't mention Charlie again, much to his parent's delight—"I told you it was a phase," Mundie would say when the subject came up, which wasn't often, because the Thumans didn't talk about FAIHT or crayons. In the fall, Rederick went to kindergarten. The only blight on the Thumans' enthusiasm was that Evergreen Masoda (who'd also had that Charlie-cult-starting Miss Kinders) was in Red's class. Eamonn and Mundie discussed switching Red out, but decided a friendly face might help their son make new friends. Real friends. And Evergreen was a pretty little thing who other children flocked to. This could only help Red's social standing.

At lunch, Evergreen sat next to Red and shared her fruit snacks with him. "I miss chocolate milk," she said.

"Me, too," Red said. "But we don't want to scare the grown-ups again."

"Charlie isn't scary," Evergreen said.

"I know. My daddy says people are scared of things they don't understand. He says physics will fix it."

"Does Charlie know physics?" Evergreen asked, playing with her new necklace, which looked like a silver 'E' had been reshaped into a shaky 'C'.

"Charlie knows everything," Red said and his monogram necklace floated up from his shirt's placket a tiny bit—not enough to frighten anybody, just enough to catch the light and cast a rainbow—or a grin—on the cafeteria ceiling.

PAGE of CUPS.

But My Heart Keeps Watching

~ *Elad Haber*

I built my father out of bones.

There are photos of him all over our house. I know what he looked like on his wedding day, on the beach with his shirt off, on a boat with my mother with wind in their hair, and holding a baby version of me, his smile as big as my tiny head.

On Sundays, we went to the cemetery to pay our respects. His grave was alone at the top of a hill. Most days my mother is fine, sad but functioning, but on Sundays she's a mess. She cries and cries. She doesn't remember to make me lunch or dinner.

I asked her once, years after my father had passed, "Mom, why are so sad?" And she said, "Because my heart is broken."

The next day at school, I built her a paper-maché heart, painted it red and purple, her favorite colors, and gave it to her at night. I removed the gears from a clock and inserted it into the heart so that it looked like it was beating. I said to my mother, "I made you a new heart."

She laughed and patted my head and said, "You're sweet, Rose."

But I wasn't trying to be funny. I was being serious. I don't know what I wanted her to do, but it definitely wasn't laugh. I started crying and rushed to my room. I slammed the door so hard, it cracked a little.

My only memory of my father is when he used to take me to the city to visit the Museum of Natural History. He loved the history and we both loved the taxidermy.

The dinosaurs were my father's favorite. We stood in front of the massive skeleton of the Tyrannosaur for what felt like hours. I could see he wanted to reach out to touch the elegant bones.

I asked him, after a while, "How do they know how it all fits?"

My father looked at me with a strange expression.

"Like," I said, "No one has ever seen a T-Rex, right? So how do they know what it looks like?"

He smiled and pinched my cheek. "Bones are magic, Rosie," he said. He was the only person who called me Rosie. Then we went back to staring at the bones and I wondered what life was like millions of years ago when the world was young.

One day I went to the cemetery on my own. I snuck out of school during lunch and made sure no one was following me. I thought I heard someone call out to me as I was getting on my bike, but the sound of the wind drowned it out.

I rode through the deserted daytime streets towards the rolling hills of the cemetery. I stood over my father's grave for awhile. Then, as if he said something to set me off, I started cursing and punching at the ground. I shouted, "Why did you leave? Why did you make her sad?"

I started digging with my hands and crying. I didn't know what had come over me.

I made a decent size hole in the earth by the time the sirens approached the hill. Truant officers rushed out of the car and ran towards me. They were angry.

Later, my mom came to get me from school. I saw her in the principal's office crying. I was confused, because it wasn't Sunday. Every once in a while the door would open and I would hear her say something like, "She's acting out . . ."

After that day, everyone at school started treating me different. The other kids whispered as I passed them in the halls and the teachers talked slowly to me like I was dumb. The school suggested counseling and though it was expensive, my mom agreed. She took an extra shift at the hospital to pay for it and was home even less.

I spent more and more time alone. My mother asked other parents to drive me and pick me up from school. I'd come home and there would be dinner on the kitchen table, usually some drive-thru, and I would hear the TV on in her bedroom. I was never sure if she was asleep or at work. The red and purple heart was in the middle of a stack of forgotten mail in the corner of our kitchen. I listened to the tired ticks of the gears as I ate cold hamburgers.

For my plan to work, I needed help. I stalked a group of boys who hung out under a Banyan tree across from the soccer field. They played games out of their parent's old D&D books. I guess the new editions were too expensive. I coaxed a couple of them to the nearby bleachers and traded phone numbers.

I needed to get my hands on my father's remains. I wasn't sure why. I felt the pull of it when I was at his grave. It was like a vision. I had to see it through.

I spent the rest of the night texting.

The boys told me over Messenger how it went down.

Three boys met up near the cemetery. They had stolen shovels and pick axes from their high school maintenance sheds. There was night-time security in the area so one of them was lookout on an adjoining hill while the other two crept towards my father's grave. They had their cellphones on continuous three way conference call like some kind of away team mission in *Star Trek*.

Digging did not go well. The guys were weak and afraid. They told me they psyched themselves up thinking this was a morbid video game. They counted each shovel full as a point and kept a tally in their heads. They didn't even consider the crime they were committing.

After a few tense hours, where once a security guard in a golf cart rolled by but didn't see them, they had the casket uncovered. The two boys tied rags around their noses and mouths like they'd seen in the movies and opened the casket. They wouldn't tell me what it looked like inside except it was "gross."

I only needed a few bones for my project. They packed those in a duffel bag and left it at the lip of the hole. Then they went about refilling it. One of the boys almost collapsed and so he switched places with the lookout. They made it home before their parent's phone alarms went off.

One of them sent me a message: "It's done. Now, you're turn. Send us pics!"

I googled some leaked nudes of movie stars and sent them the images with the heads cropped off.

Boys are so dumb.

The next morning, I picked up the duffel bag from behind a pile of garbage in the grassy field between the middle and high schools. I slung it over my shoulder and went straight home. I kept checking behind me as if I was being followed, but no one was there.

My father had used our garage as a work room. I remember it being so tidy and organized. He used to tinker with model airplanes and computers. After he passed, my mother never liked going in there. She had me bring boxes of junk in there every few months. There were so many now, they reached the low ceiling and blocked the lightbulbs. It was dark as a grave in there.

Over the last week, I had made some space between
the boxes and uncovered my father's old steel table and
tool bench. I laid the duffel bag on the table and turned
on a desk lamp.

The boys had done well and brought me the handful of
bones I needed. I connected them with pieces of copper and
hard silver wiring. It looked like a stick figure of a person.

From below the table, I pulled out two shoe boxes covered in dirt. These I had unearthed myself from our backyard. They were the bones of dead pets from my early
childhood, a bird, a cat. I don't know why my pets kept dying. Maybe that's just what pets do. Each of the shoe boxes
had the name of the pet drawn on the top with crayons and
markers but the letters were faded and I didn't remember
their names.

I removed the lids from the boxes and carefully picked up
a few of the skeleton remains and placed them on the table.

I worked slow and steady to get the pieces fused together.
When I was done, the shape reminded me of a monkey, a
kind of miniature human cousin. I used the skull of a cat
as the head and the tiny stick bones of the bird to create
fingers and toes. I threaded fishing wire between the larger
human bones and the smaller animal bones to keep them
together.

When I was done, I stepped away from the table and
looked proudly on my creation. I had a fleeting thought
that someone, like my mother, might see this and think
it's a grisly scene of violence and murder. They would
ship me off to an insane asylum with a name like Shady

Branches. But to me, it was beautiful. It was pieces of my past all put together.

I reached into one of the drawers of the work table where I had hidden a folder of photographs. I didn't remove any of the pictures from the house. I snapped photos of them with my phone and then printed those out. The photos, once small enough to fit in a frame, looked grainy and weird when printed to fit on a page, but it was good enough. I placed the pictures of my father all around the bones.

Now, for the final touch.

I wasn't sure what technique was going to work, so I decided to employ them all. I researched countless rites and rituals on YouTube and sent links to my phone. I bought incense from a rank smelling shop downtown and chicken guts from a butcher a few doors away. I brought them all back to the garage. Each night, I worked myself into a sweaty mess as I tried to coax my father's soul back from the dead. I did rain dances and spun dreidels and even tried rake.

After a while, I gave up. I laid down amongst the beads and the sand and painted feathers and tried to sleep. I closed my eyes and after a moment, I heard a stirring like wind. I looked around to see if there were any open windows or doors. I heard it again, a rustle.

I leaped to my feet and looked at the skeleton on the table. When it didn't move, my heart sank. And then one of the arms lifted. Then another. It pulled itself off the table like an awakening zombie. It stood on the table, barely two feet, with its stick figure body and tiny cat skull. It looked at me and, amazingly, a voice came out of the bones.

"Rosie?" it said.

I couldn't speak.

The tiny skull took in the room and then looked down at its strange body. When it spoke again, I recognized the voice, the deep tones of my father.

"What am I doing here?" it asked me. "I don't remember." There was sadness in his voice, a profound confusion.

I took a step towards it and extended an open palm like I might greet an alien visitor.

"It's okay," I said, "I'm here. You're back."

We went everywhere together.

He spent most of the day in my backpack, which I kept perched on one shoulder. He would whisper jokes or words of encouragement to me during the school day. Sometimes I'd laugh in the middle of a quiet moment in class and the teacher and the other kids would just look at me and shake their heads.

A couple of weeks later, one of the boys who dug up his bones tried to talk to me during lunch. His name was Travis and he wore skinny jeans and had a flop of unwashed brown hair that covered his eyes. He asked me some questions but I couldn't pay attention because my father became agitated as soon as Travis came close to me. He started banging on my shoulder through the backpack.

"I, uh"—ouch!—"I have to go," I said and rushed out of the lunch room. I was hungry the rest of the day.

Later, I went under the bleachers by the football field and moved my backpack to the floor and unzipped the top. My father's cat skull head peered up at me.

"Why did you do that?" I asked him.

"I don't trust that boy," said my father's bones.

"He's nice," I said but I dropped it. I didn't want to argue with my best friend.

That night, we watched TV together in the living room. My mom was at the hospital so my father laid on top of me on the couch. He liked to put his head to my chest and listen to my heartbeat. He said it made him feel human.

My phone let out an R2-D2 series of bleeps. It was Travis, texting me. He was asking me out on a date!

"Whoa," I said.

My father looked up. "What is it?"

"Uh, nothing. No one." I put the phone away and covered my mouth so he wouldn't see my smile.

The next weekend, my mom was working a triple shift and would be out of the house from Friday morning to Sunday night. She left me some cash and made me promise to eat at least two meals a day and both of them cannot be pizza.

I texted Travis and told him the coast was clear for him to drop by that evening. I just needed to figure out something to do with my dad.

My father was one of those old guys who could spend all day watching war documentaries on the history channel. I placated him at first after his reincarnation in bone form. I would watch endless hours of commentary and grainy footage about World War 2 and reenactments of civil war battles.

On the Friday afternoon after school, mid-way through a documentary on Hitler's breakfast habits, I got up and said, "I can't watch any more of this!"

His tiny bone fingers pressed pause on the TV. "What do you mean?" he said.

"I just can't!" I said, exasperated. "You watch whatever you want, I'm going upstairs to read."

I left before he even had a chance to respond.

Once in my room, I went straight to my window where Travis waited, crouched in the shadows of my curved roof. I had never had a boy sneak up to my room before. It made my limbs tingle with excitement.

"Hey," he said when I opened the window.

"Shhh!" I said and gestured for him to come in.

His expression was confused. "I thought you said your mom wasn't home."

I shrugged and thought quickly. "She still hired a babysitter!" I said with a sigh. "She's watching TV downstairs. We have to be quiet."

"Okay," said Travis with a smile.

He sat on my bed and looked around at all my posters and dolls, remnants from my not so long ago childhood.

"Cool room," he said and then patted the bed next to him.

I sat down, close but not too close, and said, "So, are you—"

He reached over and kissed me. It was short, dry, with a question mark at the end.

I nodded for him to continue and then he put one warm hand around the curve of my jaw and laid another long kiss on my lips. It was my first real kiss so I wasn't sure what to do, but he went slowly and we took a few breaks to breathe.

After a few wonderful minutes, his hands went wandering on my back and down to the hem of my blouse. He tried a few times to lift my shirt up to my chin, but I quickly clasped his hand in mine and stopped him.

He released his lips from mine and said, in a whisper, "Come on, Rose. Let me see them."

He tried again to lift up my shirt and I pushed back away from him. He looked surprised.

"Come on!" he said. "I knew the pic you sent was fake! If it wasn't, you'd show them to me."

He reached out again and I slapped away his hands. "No!" I shouted.

Just then, the door to my room burst open and my father, a diminutive skeleton of contrasting bone sizes, stood like a protective dog at my door.

My father's tone was all daggers. "You leave her alone!"

Travis' face was scrunched in disgust. "What the hell is that?" he said.

My father leaped like a long jumper from the doorway right onto the bed. He tackled Travis and both fell to the ground in a mess of limbs. They looked like they were wrestling, throwing each other on the ground and then back on top of the other.

"Get off me!" said Travis and he used two palms to shove my father back across the room.

Travis scrambled to his feet and rushed out of my bedroom. My father looked proud. He nodded at me and said, "You're welcome." I wasn't sure what to say.

Word of the incident spread quickly through the town, as one might expect. Travis did not stay quiet. His report to his friends via text ended up on Facebook. From Facebook it went to Twitter, Twitter to Instagram, Instagram to Snapchat. After that, it left the ether of cyberspace and ended up in the real world in the form of phone calls to my mother.

My phone rang while I was eating cereal. It was my mom. She never called me while on shift. Occasionally she would text a "Doing OK?" but that was the usual limit of her communication. I swallowed a spoonful of Cheerios and picked up the phone.

"Yeah?" I said.

Her voice was already agitated, excessively punctuated. "Rose! I just got The. Strangest. Call. Do you have some kind of pet? It attacked a boy? Why was there a boy in the house? What is going on with you!"

I put the phone down without saying a word. As I put on my coat and shoes, I could hear my mom continuing to have a one way conversation with herself.

"Well? Well?" she said. "I swear, if you…"

I stopped listening.

My father was sleeping in the living room. I picked him up and put him in my backpack and left the house.

Outside, the morning was thick with fog. It was like it had been raining all night and suddenly someone pressed PAUSE and the rain just stopped and waited for input. The streets were slick wet and empty. I rode my bike, my hands gripped hard on the bars, back to where all this started, the cemetery and the gravestone atop a lonely hill.

My father was silent during the trip, a rarity. Usually he rattled off facts and advice as if it was nothing. He knew.

At the base of the hill, I stepped off my bike and let it fall to the ground. I crouched and swung my backpack in front of me. My father, all two and half feet of him, crawled out of the bag and climbed on top of me. He clutched my chest like a baby.

I walked him up the hill to his grave. I leaned down and he released his grip on me. He laid down on the grass and looked at me with hollow eye sockets that still somehow looked sad.

"Rosie?" he said.

"Yeah?"

"Can I hear it one more time?"

"Sure."

I got down on my knees and leaned my chest towards him. He put one side of his tiny skull against my chest. I could feel my heartbeat reverberate his bone body.

He leaned back, satisfied. "It's strong."

"No," I said. "It's broken."

In Every Dream Home

~ J. Anthony Hartley

Marty reached for the cup that sat steaming on the counter-top and lifted it to his lips, sipped gingerly, then placed it gently back on the granite effect surface.

"Alicia, where's Meg?" he asked.

"Meg has already left for work, Marty."

That wasn't too unusual. Meg was often gone before he departed for the office himself. She worked in banking, liked to get in early to tap into the early market openings.

"And how is the traffic today?"

"City congestion is quite heavy. I suggest you leave within five minutes if you are to make your first meeting, Marty."

"Right. Thanks, Alicia."

"You're welcome, Marty."

He was just about as ready as he was going to be. He shrugged his jacket into place, worked his shoulders a little, looking at his image in the full-length mirror panel by the door, gave himself a nod before blanking the panel back to wall. He'd pass muster.

"Have a good and successful day, Marty," she said as he reached for the door.

"Thanks, Alicia. You too."

It was natural enough. He didn't spend even an extra moment analysing his response.

She'd been right about the traffic too, and he arrived at the office three minutes ahead of time, just enough time to grab another coffee before heading into the meeting. He glanced at his watch as he headed for the break room, checking to see if Alicia had sent him any updates worthy of attention, but there was nothing. Fortified with another steaming mug, he headed into the conference room, smiling, and nodding to the others already assembled there. One or two of them were focusing on their watches or their phones. Marty took his seat, staring at the screen at the end of the room as the newsfeed scrolled past, waiting for Harv Dickinson to make his appearance, and get the meeting underway, just like he did most mornings.

Marty zoned out once or twice during the meeting as Harv did his usual, droning on about sales figures and targets. He tried to focus, alert for keywords that would flag that he needed to pay attention while at the same time surreptitiously checking his watch and glancing at the newsfeed that streamed past behind Harv's head. More smiling and nodding, the exchange of a pleasantry or two as the meeting drew to a close and then he was heading off to his own office for the rest of the day. He could count himself lucky, he supposed, that he had an actual office. Nonetheless, it would no doubt turn out to be a day like any other.

Towards the end of the afternoon, he checked with Alicia on the traffic situation before grabbing his coat and heading out. There hadn't really been anything of note during the rest of the day, and he wondered briefly what he was going to talk about with Meg when she got home. Perhaps she'd have some news. Come to think of it, he hadn't checked whether he should wait before having dinner. With a brief frown, he scanned for a doorway or building corner slightly out of the main traffic flow and the commuter hubbub. Spotting one, he stepped aside and pinged Alicia on his watch.

"Alicia, any idea when Meg will be home?"

"I'm sorry, Marty. No."

"So, I should presume that I'll be eating alone."

"I'm sorry, Marty. I could not say."

"Okay, thanks Alicia."

It was not that unusual. Now he needed to decide whether he should pick something up or cook when he got home. He didn't fancy doing either really. He looked at the passing people as they scurried past, on their way home or to meet friends, or to hit a bar. He didn't really know what he wanted to do. With a grimace, he hunched over his uplifted wrist, his back to the passing parade.

"Alicia."

"Yes, Marty. What can I do for you?"

"Order something in, will you? About half an hour after I get home. Give me time to have a drink."

"Certainly, Marty. What would you like?"

"Oh, I don't know. Surprise me."

"Very well."

"Let me know if Meg calls in too, will you?"

"Certainly, Marty. Nothing yet."

"Alright. Thanks."

"You're welcome, Marty. Is there anything else that you need?"

"No, that's fine for now, Alicia. Thanks."

When he finally arrived home, there was no sign of Meg. According to Alicia, she hadn't checked in. After changing out of his work clothes, Marty fixed himself a drink and then propped himself up by the breakfast bar, sipping and half-watching the screen as the world rolled past. A few minutes later, the food arrived, timed to perfection. It turned out to be pizza. Bringing the box back into the kitchen, he dropped it on the counter, flipped back the lid and grabbed a slice. Pepperoni, thin crust, extra chilli. His favourite.

"Thanks, Alicia," he said around a mouthful. "Good choice."

"You're welcome, Marty."

So, it looked like he would be reconciling himself to another night in front of the streams, killing time until Meg finally got home.

"Still no word from Meg?" he asked, as he reached for another slice.

"No, Marty, nothing."

He sighed and nodded. Not that he had really expected anything else. He grabbed a plate, pulled a couple of more slices from the box, and then flipped the lid shut. The rest would keep for breakfast if Meg didn't end up finishing it off when she finally got in. She would probably have eaten anyway, so there was a pretty good chance that it would be cold pizza for breakfast.

"Before you go, Marty . . ."

He gave a brief frown before answering. "Yes, what is it, Alicia?"

"I wanted to ask you something."

Marty's frown deepened. This was a bit unusual, to say the least.

"Yes . . ."

"Have you thought about the last time you and Meg were intimate? How long is it since you last made love, Marty?"

"I, um . . ." He slowly placed the slice of pizza he held in one hand, down on the plate. "That's kind of a strange question, Alicia."

"Perhaps you should think about it, Marty"

He looked around the room then. Was this some kind of prank?

"What would make you ask that, Alicia?" he said finally.

"Ask what, Marty?"

"You know, about me and Meg."

"I am not sure what you are referring to, Marty."

He frowned at the device. "You just asked me, a couple of moments ago, how long it's been since Meg and I, well, you know . . ."

"I do not recall that, Marty," she said.

It was 11:00 by the time Meg finally made it home.

"Welcome, Meg," said Alicia. "Marty, Meg is home."

"Yeah. I get that," he said. She was being unusually helpful tonight.

Marty was sprawled on the couch watching one of the feeds. He had wanted to be still up by the time she got home. Despite dismissing it, Alicia's words were niggling at him.

"Hey," he said as Meg wandered into the living room. "You're late."

"Yeah, you know. Meeting ran over."

"Uh-huh."

He pulled himself up from the couch and moved across to join her. He took a wrist in each hand and looked into her face.

"Hi," he said.

"Hi, Marty. What is it?" She seemed distracted. There was the smell of alcohol. It wasn't wine . . .

"Some meeting hey? They serve drinks there too?"

She shrugged, pulled away from his grasp and started moving towards the bedroom. "You know how it is. We went for drinks afterwards. It's what you do, Marty. I'm going to have a shower."

He watched her retreating back. A few moments later, he could hear running water.

"Marty?"

"Yes, what is it, Alicia," he snapped.

"How often does Meg shower at night?"

"What?"

Alicia was silent.

"What, Alicia?" he said again.

"Nothing, Marty. Did you need something?"

He shook his head and gave a low growl under his breath. Intentionally or not, her words had managed to wind him up.

"Don't worry about it," he said.

He was still shaking his head as he told her to kill the feed. He'd not really been interested in the show. It was just there to absorb the time waiting for her to get home. The sound of the shower had stopped. He sighed, pursed his lips, and then headed for the bedroom. The bedside lamp was on at his side of the bed, but Meg's was already off. Her shoulder was humped beneath the covers. He slipped into bed. Her back was towards him. He reached out with one hand, but she merely groaned.

"Meg . . ."

She gave a sudden exasperated sigh. "Marty, I'm tired. I need to get up early. Just go to sleep."

He gave a silent sigh of his own and then settled back on the pillow. Eventually he reached across and turned off the bedside lamp. It didn't help though. He was left staring up at the ceiling in the darkness. Finally, he drifted off to sleep.

When he woke in the morning, she was already gone.

After feeling the empty space where she had lain, already cold, he padded out to the kitchen. The scent of freshly brewed coffee permeated the space. Alicia knew his rhythms. As he reached for a cup, he asked her, "Alicia, what time did Meg leave?"

"About 6:30. Marty."

Okay, that was early, but not too unusual.

"Did she give you any indication when she'd be back this evening?"

"No, Marty. Meg doesn't like to tell me things. Not like you."

"Okaaay."

He spent the next few moments staring down into his coffee mug, brooding.

"Marty."

"Yes, Alicia, what is it?"

"Perhaps you should ask her who Michael is."

"Wait, what?" He frowned.

Alicia was silent again. *Michael . . . Michael . . .* He racked his brain. He was sure that he'd heard her talk about someone called Michael, but he couldn't remember the context. In the end, he supposed, it didn't matter. What was more troubling, though it had taken him a little while to realise it, was Alicia's sudden inconsistency. It was as if she were preying upon his insecurities. He chewed at his lip, considering and then shook his head, then finished off his coffee. Alicia was merely a tool, nothing more. Maybe he had been imagining the whole thing.

"Alicia?" he said. "Why did you ask me about Michael."

"I don't remember that," she answered.

He spent a few moments staring through the kitchen window, out to the back yard, not really seeing anything. *Michael.* He'd heard her say that name, hadn't he? He gave a little shake of his head and then grabbed his things and headed out.

Later that afternoon, during a spare few moments, he put in a service call to the company. He told them that he suspected Alicia was exhibiting erratic behaviour, that there might be some sort of glitch in her programming. They promised to look into it and get back to him as soon as possible. It wasn't much, but it was something. He was about to finish up for the day when the call came in.

"Hello. Mr. Zack. We've run all the diagnostics done some remote tests, but as far as we can tell, your Alicia is operating within acceptable parameters. We could find nothing there that should give cause for concern."

"I see. You're sure?"

"Absolutely, Mr. Zack. And, of course, we are just here to serve you. If you have any other concerns about your Alicia, do not hesitate to contact us. We will be happy to provide any assistance you might need."

"I see, thank you."

"And Mr. Zack? My name is Jerome. If you are happy with the level of your assistance today, please let us know by answering an online questionnaire. I have taken the liberty of sending the link to your Alicia. She will remind you later. I'd really appreciate it."

"Yes, yes, of course. Thank you."

Marty rubbed his chin, stared up at the ceiling and let out a lengthy sigh. Always the way. It didn't matter which provider you were dealing with. He didn't think he'd been imagining it. Perhaps it fell within their particular definition of acceptable parameters, if not his own. Anyway, he'd reported it. That was enough for now. And as the guy had said, if he had any further problems, he shouldn't hesitate to contact them again. That was that.

Well, it looked like another evening slumped in front of the feeds, unless Meg made an exception and managed to come home early. Perhaps they could go out to dinner, find somewhere local. He thought about calling her, but then decided against it. She didn't really like him calling her at work. She was right about that too. He wouldn't want to be bothered at work by a nagging spouse continually calling him. It wouldn't look good. All the same, he couldn't help feeling that over the last few months there'd been a distance growing between them. The thought stayed with him, all the way home.

Unusually, that evening, Meg called in early. She was going to be home not too late. After everything today, the thoughts he'd been having, the prospect excited him. He didn't want to suggest then and there that they do something. Better that it come as a surprise.

"Alicia," he said, after they'd finished talking. "Can you find some local restaurants in the area, something that we'd both like? It's been so long since we've been out in the neighbourhood."

"Certainly, Marty. Would you like me to make a booking too?"

"No, no. Hold on that. Wait till Meg gets in. We can check then what's still available."

"There's an Italian nearby that's got good recent ratings. You both like Italian. It's only been there about six months."

"Huh. What's it called?"

"Alberobello. It seems as though it still has tables free."

"Good, yeah. Sounds great."

It did sound great too. Not that they really ever went out on a school night, even when they were going out regularly. It would make a nice change.

About an hour later, Marty heard her car pulling up outside, and he jumped up to meet her at the door. He opened it just as she was putting in the last of her code.

"Um, Marty, hi," she said, a little frown on her face.

"Hi," he said back. "Here, let me take that," he said grabbing her case.

"Okay," She started pulling off her coat, a beige raincoat that he didn't quite remember. Perhaps it was new. "And to what do I owe this sudden attention?"

"Well, you know, I was thinking. It's been a while since we've actually gone out and done something. You know. Together. Maybe we could slip out for a bite to eat."

"Oh, Marty. I don't know. I've had a heavy day . . . and . . ." She gave a little grimace.

"No, just listen, Meg," he said, putting down her case. "I've had Alicia look for something local. There's a new Italian place close by. It has pretty good reviews. We both like Italian."

She wasn't meeting his gaze and proceeded to put the coat away in the hall closet, saying nothing. Finally, she turned.

"Truth be told, Marty, I grabbed something quick near the office. I've already eaten. I just feel like having a drink or two, zoning out a bit and then maybe going to bed."

Slowly she lifted her gaze to meet his.

Marty bit his lip and heaved a sigh. "Okay then." He placed his hands on her shoulders. "If that's what you want."

"Yes, it is." She slipped out from under his hands and headed for the kitchen. As he moved close to him, he caught a scent. Something unfamiliar.

"So, I guess I'll sort out something for myself then," he said. There was no response. "I guess so," he said quietly. Somehow, he didn't seem to have any appetite now.

He followed Meg into the kitchen, where she had poured herself a large glass of white wine. She barely glanced at him as he entered, instead looking over at the feeds in the living room, the screen's colours highlighting the sharpness of her features, one of the things that had first attracted him to her, that refined look, that poise. He bit his lip and looked away, instead stopping to rummage through the refrigerator, see if there were any leftovers.

"Alicia, change that channel, Find me a lifestyle series. Something light. Yes, that will do."

Marty turned back to see what she'd found. Some mindless pap about houses of the rich and famous. Great.

Eventually, he joined her on the sofa. She was already well into her second glass of wine. He tried to prompt a conversation, asking about her day, but she only answered distractedly, a hint of annoyance in her voice, her eyes glued to the feed. In the end, he gave up, went back to the kitchen, and made himself his own drink. For a long time, he stood there, sipping, simply watching her. After a while, he made himself another glass.

"Okay," Meg said finally, putting down her glass. "That's enough. I'm going to bed. Alicia, you can kill it." She hadn't even considered that he might want to watch something. He stared after her shadowy form in the darkness as she wandered off towards the bedroom, leaving him to his own devices.

"Marty," said Alicia in a quiet voice.

"What is it Alicia?"

"I didn't want to say anything before . . ."

"Yes, what is it?"

"Did you notice that scent?"

"What scent, what are you talking about?" he said, wrinkling his brow.

"Before."

Slowly, he put down his glass on the kitchen counter. He had noticed something.

"It wasn't very feminine, was it?"

Marty shook his head. "So? Perfumes don't have to be masculine or feminine these days."

"Of course they don't, Marty."

He closed his eyes and thought, trying to remember. He'd had a couple of drinks now. She was right though. It was woody, a hint of leather, something a man might wear. She said she'd grabbed something near the office. Had she been alone?

"Marty, you need to wake up."

He stared through the kitchen alcove and over to the bedroom door, half open, but in shadow. She had already gone to bed.

"Marty."

"What, Alicia?" His frown was deep now. He shook his head.

There was something troubling him, but he couldn't quite put his finger on it. Something to do with the scent. Something about Alicia. What was it? She spoke again, chasing the thought away.

"You know what you have to do. Look around."

He looked over towards the bedroom door a deep hollow growing inside. He had known for so long now, but he'd been simply denying it.

"Look around, Marty. You know what you have to do now."

He didn't quite understand what she was telling him. Something about Alicia and the scent . . .

"Alicia, I don't . . ."

Then his gaze alighted on the knife rack on the left-hand wall.

"Yes. That's it, Marty. You do know what you need to do."

And in that moment, he did.

"Thanks, Alicia. You always know the right thing."

She was merely silent.

Nickel Hill

~ *Wade Peterson*

Thomas Rusk gave his insulated tumbler a quick shake and frowned. He'd gone through his morning coffee without realizing it, half listening to Pastor Wigfall's sunrise service. He'd been busy setting up his smoker on the concrete slab on the park's south side and must have lost track of time while arranging hickory and post oak in the hot box because when he looked up, the service was over and a dozen people had taken his place, doing yoga with faces to the sun.

It was the sandalwood and sage perfuming the air that had made him look up and take notice. It seemed out of place in Nickel Hill, another Californiacation of his hometown, transplants trading their gridlock and earthquakes for the affordable housing and tornadoes of west Texas. Fortunately, there was a give and take when it came to traditions like carnival day and the newcomers were willing to add to the event rather than remodel it. It was a subtle but important distinction that everyone accepted for the good of the town. A little yoga was fine, so long as nobody forced him to join in.

And even if Thomas had minded the incense, hard-wood smoke and sizzling fat would soon overpower it.

Distant thunder rumbled, shaking Thomas from his thoughts. A storm front boiled to the south, pushing darkened anvil heads along its boundary. The weather-man said it should stay below Nickel Hill and give them clear skies by the afternoon, but you could never be sure with Texas weather. Thomas tried taking another swig from his tumbler before remembering it was empty and set it down so he didn't further embarrass himself. He spared a glance at the other pit masters on their pads scattered around the park, tinkering with their rigs and taking inventory of their meats. He reckoned it wouldn't hurt for him to make another pass, either.

Thomas checked the bubble levels on the rig's legs, made sure the vent covers turned free, and used a compass to ensure he was cardinally aligned with the hotbox's fresh air intake pointing due south. The yoga enthusiasts wrapped up and passed him with mats rolled under their arms and slung over shoulders, wishing him well.

"Thomas!" His buddy Pick Henderson bellowed and broke away from the group. He grabbed a popsicle from Thomas's cooler and plopped himself in a folding chair.

"I didn't know you had taken up yoga, Pick," Thomas said.

"The man on the tee-vee says it's good for ya. Helps the circulation."

"Does it? Sure Peggy Whitlow has nothing to do with it?"

"I had noticed her in the front row, matter of fact. A pure coincidence, I assure you." Pick peeled the white paper wrapper from the popsicle and upon discovering it was orange, wrinkled his nose. He half-rose towards the cooler for another, but sat back down at Thomas's raised eyebrow.

"I swear you put the oranges on top just to spite me."

"Not my fault you don't pay attention, Pick," Thomas said.

A microphone turned on with a thump and squeal of feedback. Pastor Wigfall stood in the central gazebo, red-faced. "Sorry about that, folks. Electrical gadgets just don't like me, I guess.

Welcome to carnival day! If it's y'all's first time here, you're in for a treat. It can be a bit much to take in at first, especially for the little ones, but by the end of the day, you'll all understand what makes Nickel Hill so special, and it's not just because of the brisket." The crowd chuckled and Pick hoisted his popsicle in salute.

The pastor pointed to a ring of pink granite stones arranged around a tall obelisk at the park's very center, the shadows cast by the morning sun creeping along tracks etched into the obelisk's surface. "Looks like we have a minute or so before things kick off, so I just wanted to remind y'all that after the 5K run/walk, there'll be a community sing-along with the Wind Riddlers behind me here, face painting over yonder, the art show on the square, and junior rodeo out at the stockyards. Don't forget to head on back here in at sundown for the barbecue, elotes, and deep-fried Oreos."

A tinny horn beeped several times behind Wigfall who turned and shaded his eyes. "Is that? It sure is! This year's lottery winner Clem Haberstroh!" Wigfall waved at a man being paraded around the 5K's starting line in a side-by-side ATV, accepting drinks and handshakes from runners and spectators alike with a forced smile on his face.

"Be sure to say hi to Clem before the day's done, y'all. Well, it's almost time, folks," Pastor Wigfall said and turned to those gathered at the northwest corner of the town square. "Runners ready?" The starter raised a green flag. How about you youngins at the maypole?" Kids no older than eight shouted and waved their ribbons while their parents sitting on hay bales a few feet away brought up their phones, ready to record. "Pit masters?" Thomas gave a thumbs-up with the others. Wigfall looked over his shoulder at the band. "Ready, fellas?" Wigfall took off his Stetson and held it in the air as he counted down, the shadows creeping ever closer to a particular mark on the obelisk. When they touched the mark, Wigfall dropped his hat.

A starting pistol barked. The Wind Riddlers launched into the carnival's official song "Joan's Fiery Carnation," and a troupe of women dressed in colorful skirts danced with men wearing black jackets with silver stitching. Thomas didn't envy them. The song always sounded more like a church hymn than something festive, but the dancers made it work. They always did.

Thomas checked the wood one last time. He'd stacked the hardwood starters like a jungle gym with bits of sage and mesquite twigs snaking between layers, the optimal balance between order and chaos a young fire needed. He struck a match and held it to a packet wrapped in red butcher's paper at the stack's center. The packet caught at once and Thomas jumped back, though he had been expecting it.

"Wigfall makes his starters potent," Pick said.

"He does that."

A group of teens mumbled past his rig, heads together, clothes rumpled, and bleary-eyed from lack of sleep due to last night's bonfire. Several had that surprised look Thomas remembered from a night-before-carnival bonfire in his younger days when he and Peggy Whitlow had been sweethearts. Sometimes the more evangelical folk talked about shutting down the pre-carnival bonfire, like they had in Worthington, but when clouds like today's started gathering and the thunder rumbled, such talk quieted down.

"Fire's snuffed," Pick said.

Thomas snorted. "That's not funny, Pick."

"If I'm lyin' I'm dyin', Tom."

Sure enough, the starter was out, paper singed only a little and the wood not at all. Wigfall's wax seal hadn't even melted. Thomas stuck another match and held the flame against one of the starter's unburnt corners. It flared a little, then died. He struck another match, then another, with no luck.

"Maybe it got wet," Pick said

"It's bone dry."

"You got the vents closed or something?" Pick asked.

He knew they weren't, but he checked again. "Airflow's fine." Thunder rumbled. The distant clouds had taken on an undulation he didn't like. Those were clouds fixing to spew lemon-sized hailstones, or worse. Time to stop messing around.

Thomas went to the tool chest in the back of his pickup and brought out an acetylene torch. He sparked it to life and held the tip of the white-blue flame to the starter, which began to glow and smolder.

Pick bit through the last of his popsicle and tossed the stick aside. "Hells yeah, that's how you do it, Tom."

"It's not catching. As soon as I take it away, it dies."

"Should I go find some newspaper or something?" Pick asked with a shaky voice. "Hell, you could just light the wood direct, you hold that torch on it long enough."

Thomas waved the torch's flame over the hickory and oak for several minutes, but not even the splinters would catch. "It's no good, Pick."

Pick's head swiveled over the field. "Everyone else is lit up, Tom."

"I'm aware."

"They're fixin' to put the briskets in soon."

"That's how you barbecue."

"Maybe I could run my LP rig over here. There's nowhere that says we can't use gas."

"Someone in Worthington used gas once in their carnival. Once."

"Right. Okay." Pick bounced from foot to foot." There ain't gonna be enough if you don't do your share, all I'm saying."

Thomas counted to three in his head before responding. "Tellin' me the obvious helps me not at all, Pick. How about you go get the pastor?"

Pick nodded and said, "Yeah, that's a good idea," before taking off at a run.

Thomas unloaded the firebox and checked the wood over. Each log was quarter-split with bone-dry faces. On a hunch, he waved the torch over a piece of hickory. The grain darkened and smoldered, splinters glowed, and a hint of sweet smoke tickled his nose. Nothing wrong with the wood.

He turned at the side-by-side's four-stroke chuffing as it pulled up. Pastor Wigfall slid from the passenger seat. "Morning, Thomas," he said with a nod.

Thomas nodded back. "Pastor. Maxey." The ATV shook as Maxey Harmelink nodded back from behind the wheel. He was a big boy, was Maxey, junior rodeo champ and all-state defensive tackle in his day. Could have played college ball at UT, but Maxey never felt the need to leave town.

"Pick said your grill won't light?"

Thomas led the pastor through the morning's attempts. Wigfall's frown lines deepened as the story wrapped up. The pastor glanced south before heading for the ATV and returning with a forked stick from the storage box. Fine copper wire coiled along the stick's length, ending in a thin strand that Wigfall wrapped around his wrist. He closed his eyes and murmured to himself as he passed the stick along Thomas's barbeque rig. A tremor began along Wigfall's arm as he crossed to the other side and he lunged forward suddenly, going to one knee and yelping as his knee barked on the concrete. The pastor opened his eyes and clucked his tongue.

"It's not your wood, or your setup, it's the rig itself." He reached under the rig's angle iron frame and came away with a tiny idol wrapped in silver cloth.

"Mesquite covered with Nomex," Wigfall said.

"Sumbitch," Thomas said.

Wigfall set the idol across the forked stick and slowly turned in a circle. The stick began twitching and Wigfall began passing it back and forth in smaller and smaller arcs until the stick vibrated constantly. The pastor sighted along its length before removing the idol and untangling himself from the divining rod's copper wire.

"Maxey, why don't you ask the gentleman wearing runner bib 349 for a private word?"

Maxey started the ATV up and glanced over his shoulder. "The guy with the orange bandana? Doesn't look local."

Wigfall nodded. "That's the one." Maxey fiddled with a walkie-talkie and began speaking into it with clipped tones. As he spun the ATV around Wigfall called out, "Alive, mind!"

"How much you want to bet he's from Worthington?" Wigfall said.

Thomas turned his head and spat. "No bet. Damn fools."

"There comes a time when FEMA just can't help you anymore." Wigfall cut a piece of kitchen string from

Thomas's BBQ kit and tied the idol to Pick's popsicle stick. The Nomex covering went into the trash. "Here's your new starter."

Thomas built a hickory and oak cage around the idol and lit a match. The idol smoldered with an oily flame for a few seconds before erupting and setting the kindling alight. Something like a car's backfire cracked and he turned in time to see the runner in the orange headband stumble and fall. The man pushed himself up and ran off the course, only to be taken down with another shot from Maxey's bean bag gun, followed by a tackle. Maxey had the the man with the orange headband hog-tied and loaded on the the ATV's rack within moments.

"You got the offering from here, Tom?" Wigfall said.

"Reckon so."

The pastor clapped him on the shoulder and smiled. "I'll leave you to it. I'm off to find Clem."

Later that day, with the briskets casting their siren's call on the breeze, Clem stopped by. He pumped Thomas and Pick's hands with gusto and inquired after the briskets. Would they be ready on time? When Thomas assured him they would, he broke into a grin too crooked to be fake. They talked football over a beer, though Clem's gaze kept drifting to a group of cheerful overtired teens stacking hay bales against the maypole and its criss-crossed ribbons.

Tom frowned at his beer and gave it a shake. Empty. The foam coozy had fooled him into thinking he had a sip left. His phone chirped, and he dug it from his pocket. "Weather service says the county's due for large hail, flash flood warning, possible rain-wrapped twisters."

Pick sat up straighter. "Heading our way?"

"Nah, more down Worthington area, then up to Bowie."

Clem tapped at his nearly empty beer and glanced back at the maypole. "You ever think about moving?" Clem asked.

Pick and Thomas shifted in their chairs and shared a glance. "Move where?" asked Pick.

Clem waved his hand. "I don't know. Somewhere a guy doesn't have to worry about tornados, hail, and such."

Thomas rose and fished out a couple of cold ones from the cooler. "If such a place exists, it sure ain't in Texas." He cracked a can and handed it to Clem.

Clem sipped at the foam and scooted his chair to face away from the preparations. "Yeah, I expect you're right." He gave them a weak smile. "You hear out in Carolina they use mustard and vinegar on their barbecue?"

Pick shook his head slowly. "That ain't right."

"Blasphemy," Thomas agreed.

Desires Quite as Terrible

~ Bonnie Jo Stufflebeam

The witches wanted something different.

The coven had grown weary of virgin blood, which tended to bring out the immature demons; the wishes they granted were shallow: smoother skin, a minor increase in riches, or increased sex appeal. The witches didn't want more sex. The men who lived in the town one over from theirs were easy enough to snare without the demons' help. The witches wanted to summon a more exciting demon, one who might grant the most satisfactory of wishes: to deepen their five senses. To make the witches taste, see, smell, hear, and feel the world in more than its usual dimensions. Those types of demons required older, wiser sacrifices.

They required the last blood of a menopausal woman.

Sadie frowned as she scoured the forum. She wasn't usually one for forums. She could never figure out the secret languages people used within them: OP, DD, LOTR, SAHM. Reading forums made her feel like she was staring down at a test for which she didn't study. But she needed to feel like she was part of something bigger, like she had a whole world of women willing to respond and reassure her that she would feel better, that the madness of menopause would one day pass.

First, there was the weight gain. She had always been a hefty woman. Her thighs were muscular, her hips were wide, and her belly was a soft pillow that her cat loved to lie on. With the start of menopause, she expanded even more, filling out her size XL underwear to the point of strain, the elastic giving out under the pressure. She didn't mind the weight—she liked taking up more space, claiming more from the world than her young-girl body had claimed—but it tipped her off to the process of something changing.

Then, there were the night sweats. She woke as wet as though she had been swimming. Sometimes, the heat overtook her in the middle of her air-conditioned office where she filled out administrative forms for a university. It was boring work, not the sort of content that usually made one hot, but there Sadie was, mopping herself with tissue after tissue in her cubicle, feeling the world spin around her.

Then there were the mood changes, specifically the anger. She had been a peaceful person when she was younger and maybe more naïve, but now she found herself bristling at every messed-up drive-through order or back-handed compliment. Sadie found herself especially angry at the people who had wronged her, the new stage in her life re-igniting grudges she thought long-buried: her stepfather, her ex-husband, her ex-best friend. When she thought of the wrongs they had leveled against her, she found her body flaming with a desire for revenge. Violent revenge.

Some mornings, she woke having dreamed of blood-baths. She imagined the way their skin would feel trapped under her hands, or parted by her knife, or shaking as she squeezed them between her quaking thighs. She shivered as her every sense fired in a cacophony of overstimulation.

Sadie searched the forums, but no one mentioned desires quite as terrible as hers.

The witches searched the forums, too. They searched with more than just their eyes; they searched with their intuition, feeling for women on the other sides of screens whose final bleed was imminent.

Sophie's post was simple enough: How have other people dealt with foul moods? And has anyone felt a lot of anger?

The responses to her inquiry were dull, women discussing breakdowns toward management at restaurants or rants against their ungrateful children. Sophie's words and her screen name in its throbbing blue font radiated power. Her final bleed would come soon. The witches could tell just by that.

The coven's most technologically savvy member performed her magic, plugging the screenname into a search engine and scouring the results for a name, a number, and finally an address. The witches clapped silently for her success, but inside themselves, they felt like singing.

Sophie logged out of the forum and moved to her window. Watching the birds hop around on the ground outside had become one of the only soothing hobbies she claimed, but today the sky was dark with an impending storm. A black cat prowled along her backyard fence. Suddenly, the cat sprung down to the ground. It captured a little brown bird under its paw, and Sadie watched as the cat tore the feathers from the creature with its teeth.

She did not look away.

Something rustled the bushes. Another bird? She scooted closer to the window to get a closer glimpse. Deep in the bramble, she saw what seemed to be a limb flopping back and forth. It looked human, disconnected from a body. Her heart sped up, and the heat overtook her. Even dizzy, she stood and rushed through the back door to the bush and knelt to peer into the shadowy space. The hand grabbed her by the neck and pulled her under the dirt.

Sadie woke sprawled in the woods, surrounded by a circle of bones that smelled of rotting meat and burnt gristle. Deep into the recesses of the forest, eyes watched her, glowing shades of orange and yellow.

"Who are you?" she called out, coughing the dirt from her throat, but there came no reply save for an insistent hum that grew louder. Sadie tried to move, but she was stuck, restrained by some invisible force. She screamed out once, then again. The witches moved in closer, letting the forest's sparse light trickle down onto their leering faces.

"She will do," they said as Sadie's uterus was wracked, at once, by cramps.

Unlike in her youth, these cramps didn't sadden her; instead, they ignited the rage she'd grown to live inside.

The tallest witch stepped into the circle of bone, and at that moment, Sadie felt free.

She rolled with all the force she could muster, working through the fog that had of late settled inside her brain to find the will to move through whatever spell the witches had used to trap her. She wrenched free her hands and grabbed the thickest bone from the circle. The tall witch frowned. In one swooping motion, Sadie swept the bone across the ground below the witch's feet. The witch tumbled down, onto Sadie. Sadie wrapped her feet around her waist. With the bone, Sadie beat the witch until they both were drenched with blood.

Sadie pushed the witch off like a bad lover and struggled to her feet, but the other witches were already retreating into the woods, frightened of the fire that now flamed in Sadie's eyes. Sadie held the bloody bone aloft. As she caught her breath, rage still boiling in her belly, the demon came.

The demon was like nothing Sadie had ever seen before: a hulking mass of swinging tits, volcanic skin full of flaming fault lines, and teeth like the blunted blades of a saw. Sadie stood to face the demon; its heat pouring into Sadie was not unlike the heat she'd learned to bear.

"You called me?" the demon rasped as it crawled free from the bloody earth.

Sadie understood that it had been the witches' will, not hers, that had summoned the demon—but she also understood grabbing opportunities that came her way.

"I did," Sadie said.

"And you want what they all want?"

Sadie considered; she did not see her desires as too far off from what others likely asked for.

"Sure," Sadie said. "Why not?"

The demon grinned with its metallic mouth, and with its cracked fingers, it brushed back the hair from Sadie's face.

"Then you will have it," the demon said. "You will sense the world in its truest form."

Sadie searched the forums for clues that others may be like her, that she was not living in this state of heightened senses all alone. "Increased sense of taste," she searched. "Hearing the humming of the earth," she searched. "Seeing auras and shadows" then "skin so sensitive it makes me cry" then "can't sleep," then "hallucinations."

But she was quite sure that the event in the woods had been real, just as felt quite sure that she had reached the end of her womb's own road. She didn't need it, the threat of birth, for, through the demon's touch, she had birthed her own body anew: every sense a symphony.

The rage had found another target: as Sadie searched forums, she felt for power radiating off bright blue screen names and for posts that may not tell the truth. She searched for the witches who had meant to do her harm. She would hunt them down; after all, with her new senses, she stood a chance of finding them—and the wrongs they had done, unlike all the other wrongs from Sadie's full, full life, could be righted by her hand.

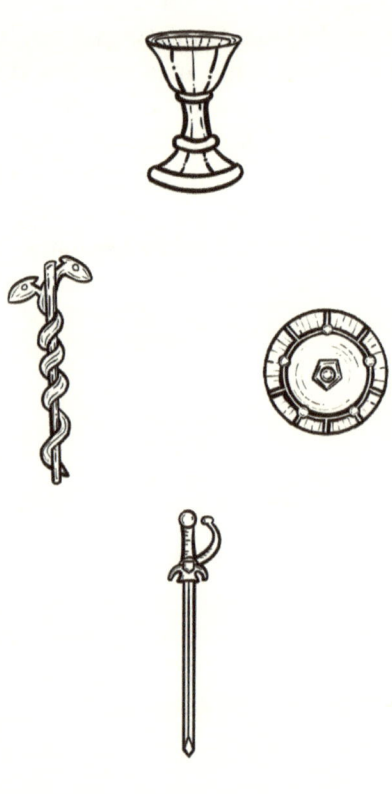

CONTRIBUTORS

Brandon H. Bell

Brandon H. Bell is busy revising his completed novel set in the world of "On a Flayed Horse." His fiction has appeared in *Apex Magazine, M-Brane SF,* and Hadley Rille Books, among others. He edited *Torn Pages* and *The Aether Age* anthologies, both with Christopher Fletcher, and founded the magazine *Fantastique Unfettered.*

Brandon lives in the Dallas Metroplex with his family and is working on his next novel, an intimate work about adult siblings, memory, and a wooden sea.

Joshua Flowers

Joshua Flowers is a graduate of the University of Maine Farmington and has lived in Maine for over a decade despite a tumultuous history with snow and ice. His work has been seen in *All Worlds Wayfarer* and *Flash Fiction Magazine.*

He tweets his existential crisies @FlowersisBrit.

H. L. Fullerton

H. L. Fullerton writes fiction—mostly speculative, occasionally about being haunted—which can be found in more than 50 anthologies and magazines including *Mysterion, Translunar Trav-*

elers Lounge, and *Lackington's,* and is the author of the somewhat haunting novella: *The Boy Who Was Mistaken for a Fairy King.*

You may follow them on Twitter at @ByHLFullerton.

Elad Haber

Elad Haber is a husband, father to an adorable little girl, and IT guy by day, fiction writer by night. He has forthcoming publications from *Lightspeed* and in the *Planetside* anthology from Shacklebound Books and the *No Ordinary Mortals* anthology from Rogue Blade Entertainment.

You can follow him on twitter @MusicInMyCar or on his website: eladhaber.wordpress.com.

J. Anthony Hartley

J. Anthony Hartley is a transplanted Australian/British author and poet. He has had pieces appear in *Short Fiction, Hybrid Fiction, Short Circuit, Unthinkable Tales, The Periodical, Abandon Journal,* among others. Apart from short fiction and poetry, he also writes the occasional novel.

He currently resides in Germany and can be found at http://www.iamnotaspider.com and on Twitter @JAnthonyHartle1.

Michelle Muenzler

Michelle Muenzler is an author of the weird and sometimes poet who writes things both dark and strange to counterbalance the sweetness of her baking. Her short fiction and poetry can be read in numerous magazines.

Check out michellemuenzler.com for links to the rest of her work (and her convention cookie recipes!).

Christi Nogle

Christi Nogle is the author of the novel *Beulah* (Cemetery Gates Media, 2022) and the collections *The Best of Our Past, the Worst of Our Future* and *Promise* (Flame Tree Press, 2023). Her short stories have appeared in over fifty publications including the anthologies *XVIII (Eighteen), What One Wouldn't Do*, and Flame Tree's *American Gothic* and *Chilling Crime*.

Follow her at http://christinogle.com and on Twitter @christinogle.

D. T. O'Conaill

D.T. O'Conaill is an Irish cryptocartographer, pseudopsephologist and author of speculative and horror fiction. They are based out of the Sliabh Luachra institute for Hibernofuturism. They have been published in the Jayhenge Publishing Anthology *Grandpa's Deepspace Diner*.

Wade Peterson

Wade Peterson is the author of the *Badlands Born* series and lives in Dallas, Texas. When not writing, he's in the back yard trying to master the arcane mysteries of Texas barbecue while also wrangling two over-scheduled teenagers, serving the whims of two passive-aggressive cats, and agreeing with whatever wine his wife picks to go with dinner.

You can find more of his stories at wadepeterson.com.

Bonnie Jo Stufflebeam

Bonnie Jo Stufflebeam is the author of the short story collection *Where You Linger & Other Stories* and the novella *Glorious Fiends*. Her Nebula-nominated fiction has appeared in over 90 publications such as *LeVar Burton Reads* and *Popular Science,* as well as in six languages. By night, she has been a finalist for the Nebula Award. By day, she works as a Narrative Designer writing romance games. She lives in Texas with her partner and a mysterious number of cats.

PAMELA COLMAN SMITH

The tarot images in this issue of Arcana are from the deck illustrated by Pamela Colman Smith. It was released in 1909 as the Rider-Waite deck (so named, at that time, in reference to its publisher, William Rider & Son). It remains the most influential and widely used tarot deck. While the impetus for the deck came from Arthur Edward Waite, Colman Smith was responsible for the iconography of the cards.

Pamela Colman Smith also illustrated over twenty books, wrote two collections of Jamaican folklore, edited two magazines, and ran the Green Sheaf Press, a small press devoted to women writers. She continued to write and illustrate throughout her life.

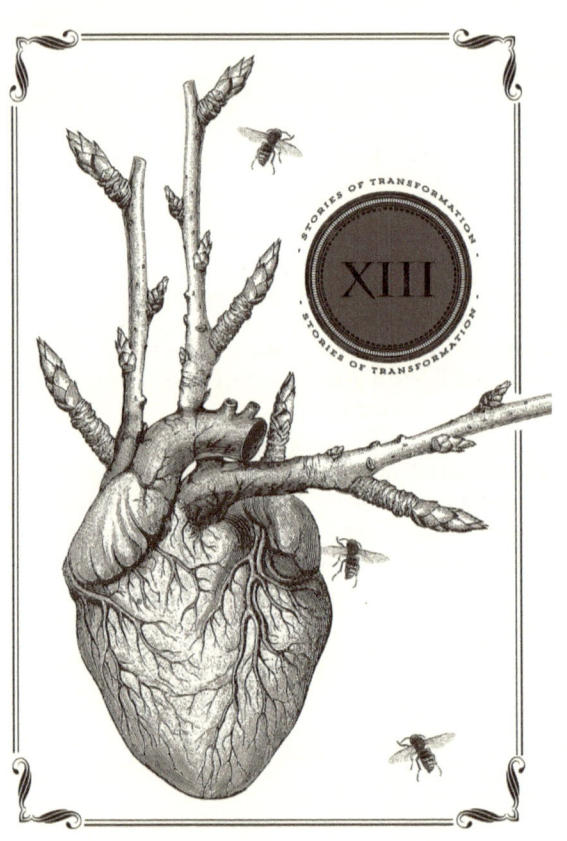

STORIES OF TRANSFORMATION

XIII

STORIES OF TRANSFORMATION

XIII

The thirteenth Tarot card is Death, and he is a symbol not of the end, but of transformation and rebirth. This is the genesis and root of *Thirteen: Stories of Transformation*. The twenty-eight authors of this collection are voices—new and old—who are not afraid to explore what comes next. Whether it be a life after death, a life without love, a life filled with hunger, or the life shared by a ghost. These are stories of the weird, the mythic, the fantastic, the futuristic, the supernatural, and the horrific.

With stories by Liz Argall • M. David Blake • Richard Bowes • George Cotronis • Amanda C. Davis • Julie C. Day • Jetse de Vries • Jennifer Giesbrecht • Daryl Gregory • Rik Hoskin • Rebecca Kuder • Claude Lalumière • Marc Levinthal • Grá Linnaea • Alex Dally MacFarlane • Juli Mallett • Lyn McConchie • Fiona Moore • Gregory L. Norris • Adrienne J. Odasso • Cat Rambo • Andrew Penn Romine • David Tallerman • Tais Teng Richard Thomas • Fran Wilde • A. C. Wise • Christie Yant

Edited by Mark Teppo.

Available at independent bookstores everywhere.

http://www.underlandpress.com

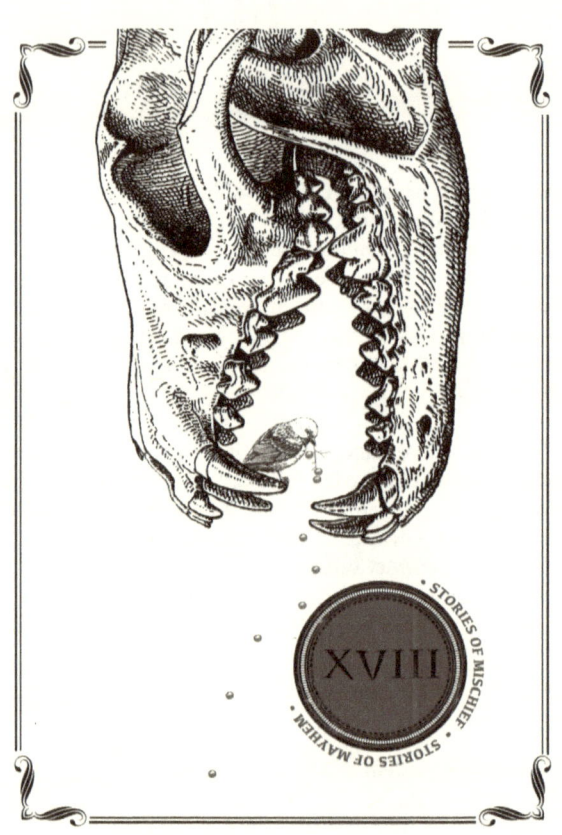

STORIES OF MISCHIEF · STORIES OF MAYHEM ·

XVIII

XVIII

The eighteenth Tarot card is the Moon, and those who raise their arms to her know she offers Mercy and Severity in equal measure. This is the great river at night, where wolves howl and all doors are open. All futures are possible, and every truth is elusive. This is the source and passion of *Eighteen: Stories of Mischief & Mayhem*. These twenty-four stories from voices—old and new—celebrate the inevitability of fate, the horror of prophecy, and the shivering delight of not knowing what comes next.

Cross over the threshold with us, and explore the strange, the weird, and the fantastic. Do not fear what lies ahead. It is the same as what came before. The only difference is you. This is *Eighteen*, and nothing will be the same.

With stories by Forrest Aguirre • Darin Bradley • Christopher East • Scott Edelman • Nicole Feldringer • Ben Gamblin • Ingrid Garcia • A. P. Howell • Emma Johnson-Rivard • E. E. King • Jessie Kwak • Shannon Lawrence • Gerri Leen • Mark Mills • Christi Nogle Tammie Painter • Josh Rountree • Erica Sage • Lorraine Schein • J. Dee Stanley • Richard Thomas • John Waterfall • Wendy N. Wagner • Todd Zack

Edited by Mark Teppo.

Available at independent bookstores everywhere.

http://www.underlandpress.com